The Outlaw League

The Outlaw League

Lance Woolaver

Illustrated by
P. John Burden

NIMBUS
PUBLISHING

Nimbus Publishing Limited
P.O. Box 9301, Station A
Halifax, N.S.
B3K 5N5

Design Editor: Kathy Kaulbach
Project Editor: Alexa Thompson

Nimbus Publishing Limited gratefully acknowledges the support of the Council of Maritime Premiers and the Department of Communications.

Canadian Cataloguing in Publication Data

Woolaver, Lance, 1948-

The outlaw league

(New Waves)

ISBN 0-921054-71-8

I. Burden, P. John, 1942- . II. Title. III. Series.

PS8595.064097 1991   jC813'.54   C90-097705-1
PZ7.W660u 1991

Printed and bound in Canada

This book is dedicated to Joe Potter's Dad,
Keith, and to Joe Potter too.

Contents

1
The Line-up

I can see the Tiger at the end of the field, where the shade from the summer trees falls across the long, green grass. I want the Tiger. Got to have him. Looks to me like the Tiger is sleeping. I wonder.

Maybe he is awake, watching me. I shift my gear off my shoulder. Are his eyes shut? Maybe he is just squinting in the sun. I take my time, coming across the field by the ditch. When I get near, I say, "Tiger?"

I give the sleeping Tiger a kick on the kneecap with the toe of my sneakers. This is a bad move. It hurts.

The Tiger opens his eyes. "Nicky Come-Play-Ball," he says. That's what he calls me. "How are we doing?"

"OK," I say. "It's time to play ball."

"I've been here since ten," the Tiger says.

"You didn't get out of bed till ten. I talked to your sister."

"What does she know?"

"She knows you."

The Tiger looks up into the tree branches. He is chewing gum. His head is in the shade, but his legs and feet are in the bright sunlight. The red dust of the field is all over his sneakers and pants. He's been hitting rocks with his bat, because there are all these little nicks and cuts in the bat. His ball glove is in the crook of the tree. He is ready to play ball.

"Give me an orange."

I have four oranges from home, stuck in my pockets. The idea is that I will cut them up for the team, at the game. I need the Tiger now, so I give him one.

"How many players have we got?"

"Seven, counting you. And we can get Ronnie Wong and Mei-Ling, at the Café."

"Oh, geez."

The Tiger doesn't like to play baseball with

girls. He will play stinger-miss or catch-it-on-the-bounce with girls, but not baseball.

"She can field better than you can."

"Good field, no hit," the Tiger says. "She can't hit worth...."

The Tiger is looking for a real good word.

"Don't swear," I say.

"Real ballplayers swear. Real ballplayers swear a lot."

"Ballplayers chew real tobacco."

The Tiger thinks, but not for long.

"I can hit," the Tiger says. He looks disgusting—his cheeks are puffed out like a chipmunk's. His face is dusty from hitting all those rocks on this red-dirt field. Orange juice dribbles down his chin and drips onto his shirt, leaving little tracks in the dust on his face like raindrops racing down a window pane.

"I can hit," he says, as if this answers everything.

"Great! Put you and Mei-Ling together and we've got one whole ballplayer."

"Put me and anybody together and we'll win the game. Who're we playing?"

"South End."

The Tiger sags, because if we play the South End team it means we have a long walk.

"If we get Ronnie and Mei-Ling now, my Uncle Teddy will still be at the Long Wharf. He'll give us a lift."

"In the clam truck?"

"It's better than walking."

The Tiger is not too crazy about the clam truck, especially on a hot day.

"Who've we got, anyways?"

"We've got you to start, Freddy catching, Bubby Neville on first, Dougie Van Tassel in left, Howard in centre and Jimmy Christmas in right. Put me on second, Ronnie on third, and Mei-Ling at short—good arm, good glove. Airtight, eh? "

"Dougie Van Tassel is on his paper route. I saw him."

"He says he'll be there. Even if he isn't, we've still got eight."

"We can't beat South End with eight," the Tiger says.

"With you pitching, we can." I say this

because the Tiger likes to be encouraged.

The Tiger leans over and beats the dust off his pants. We walk into town to pick up Ronnie and Mei-Ling. They live over the Café. We will pick up Freddy and Bubby on the way. Hopefully the outfield is already on the wharf with my Uncle—if not, they'll have to walk.

We make it to the Long Wharf in good time. My Uncle Teddy is taking off soon for the clam flats; the tide is on the way out and most of the dories are already sitting on the mud. His sled and tubs, clam hack and boots are in the back of the truck. There is one *terrible* smell coming from that truck.

The Tiger gives me his worst "oh, that clam truck" look, and I give him my "it's better than walking" look.

"Yeah," he admits grudgingly, "he could be coming back from the clam flats with those tubs full of unshucked clams for us to ride around with."

"We'll sit up front," I tell the Tiger.

The Tiger is happy with that. I am happy to have the Tiger where he should be, which is on

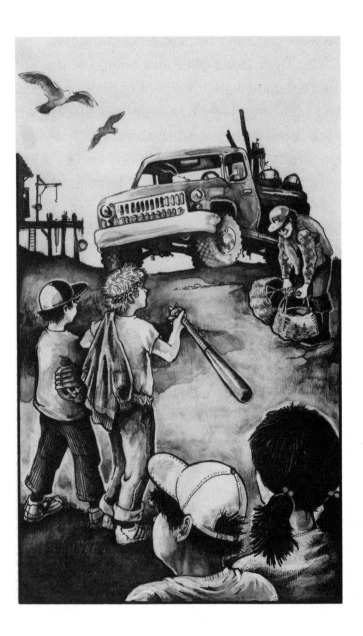

his way to pitch a ball game for the Ravens.

The Tiger rolls up his window so the smell from the clam tubs won't get in the cab. I sit in the middle with my knees up in my face, feet and elbows wrapped around the stick shift, watching the telephone poles slip by. The Tiger looks back over his shoulder at Ronnie and Mei-Ling sitting in the box of the truck. It is pretty crowded back there, with the outfield— Dougie, Howard and Jimmy. The Tiger laughs, and we are off to the ball game.

2

The Tiger and Mei-Ling
Do Not Have a Discussion

It's the bottom of the fifth with two outs.

The sun has gone behind the clouds and now these big, black thunderclouds are rolling in off the Bay. If we get the out, and it rains, we'll win.

It's a rule: if you play five full innings before you're rained out, that's a legal game.

We are up one run, 3-2. I am praying for rain.

You can see the ball really well now, because of the dark sky and also because the Tiger is slowing down. Still, I feel good about our chances, until Ronnie's throw off an infield roller goes sailing straight into right field. If he had an arm he'd be dangerous.

I'm on the mound talking to the Tiger when

the raindrops start to patter on the dust of the infield.

So far so good.

"Condemned to die," the Tiger says. He's talking about the batter.

"Well, we don't beat these guys too often," I say by way of apology for coming to the mound to suggest he should come out. "I just thought that maybe we might bring in Freddy to mop up. If we can get a fly ball we're out of here. His arm is rested."

"It can keep on resting," the Tiger says. "Besides, three strikes and the game is over." I can see he's sweating. In the cool of a summer shower, he is sweating.

The Tiger holds out his palm. Little raindrops splash on his arm.

If we stand here talking, and the rain really does come down, it won't be a game. It won't go in the book as a win. We don't really have a book, but it wouldn't go in it if we did.

The runner on first is dancing. The Tiger looks over at him and spits in his general direction. We both know this turkey is going nowhere. It's a rule. The ball is dead—no running when you are on the mound talking to your pitcher.

"Hey! We called time!" I say. The coach for South End tells him to get back. What a turkey this guy is, but he could be the tying run.

"*Condemned*," the Tiger says.

"OK," I say. And I don't say anything else because I don't want to jinx him.

Then everything happens in slow motion. The Tiger winds up like a rocking chair. The catcher, Freddie, rock-solid steady, settles back on his heels, waiting for the pitch. The batter is frozen, waiting. He hasn't hit the Tiger all afternoon, but he hopes this pitch is his lucky one.

We are all in the outfield, waiting. They are all in at bat, waiting. The Tiger lets it go, straight and hard. It's a rope!

Whack, crack! It's a hard hit, and slow motion cuts to fast. Suddenly, everyone is running, jumping, standing up, waving. Freddie ditches the mask, scrambles, looks up, trying to follow the ball. The Tiger spins, but the ball is past him before he can flag it down. The batter heads for first, the turkey on first base heads for second. Nuts! Then shortstop Mei-Ling darts, head down, on the ball. Sun breaks through the clouds, dark turns to light. Mei-Ling twists her hand. Backhand stab! She's got the ball!

Everything stops, except the rain. It is over! I am smiling; we win.

Mei-Ling is holding the ball up over her head. The white ball is stuck in the webbing of her glove. At first it looks as if she is crying, but it is just the raindrops on her face.

I steal a look at the Tiger—he is happy too.

The runner pulls up half way down the line. It is Bell—he is a real South Ender. He must have six baseball gloves. He's got real baseball shoes; spikes! He laughs....

"I hit that hard," Bell says.

And he did, but that doesn't change anything. We won!

Walking in from the field, I say to the Tiger, "Good pitch."

The Tiger knows what I am thinking. "She can field," he says. "I never said she couldn't field. But I can pitch. I can hit...."

"You set a world's record for dying on third."

"Not my fault."

We shake hands with the South Enders. They are so clean! They're cleaner after the game than we were before it started! The rain is really coming down now, so we hustle to pick up the bases.

"Good game, good game ... good game."

"Next time, nine innings."

"Yeah," the Tiger says, "and we'll beat you by twice as much."

The Tiger enjoys his wins.

We start to leave. The South Enders have a lift home in their new van. Their coach is driving them. He's a new guy in town and this is his van. He doesn't talk much to us, and he doesn't offer us a lift.

Go ahead, pal. You play, but you don't stay. I am hoping Uncle Teddy doesn't show up in the clam truck. A wet clam truck is something awful to smell, like the mudflats by the fish plant at low tide. I would rather walk, even in the rain.

We get the gear together, and everybody has to carry something. Mei-Ling comes over to the plate where we are putting the catcher's gear in a canvas bag. The game ball is still stuck in the webbing of her glove. She is happy but quiet, because this is one of South End's baseballs. They have forgotten it in the rain, and the excitement. This means we have an extra baseball. Generally we only have a couple, a game ball and maybe one to practise with.

This ball was punched so far into the webbing of her glove it caught itself; she didn't even need to close on the pocket. She holds the glove out, shakes it, but the ball hangs there in the webbing. There it is, the whole ball game, in the little white ball in her wrong-handed brown glove.

I can't get over it; we won!

I am thinking that the Tiger should at least say to Mei-Ling, "Good catch!"

The Tiger thinks that Mei-Ling is showing him up by holding the baseball upside down in the glove. She sees it in his face.

"Good game, Tiger," she says, and she pulls the ball out of the webbing, her fingernails on the red-thread seams.

Her dad bought her the glove because he wanted her to play with us so she could learn good English. He didn't know that a right-hander wears the glove on the left hand, and she was so grateful to get the glove that she didn't tell him he'd made a mistake. She just wears it backwards, wrong-handed. It's worth it all. It feels so great. We won!

She flips the ball out to the Tiger as if to say, "Here it is. It's your ball game. You won it!"

I look at it, and it's a pretty good ball for a found one.

All of the Ravens are waiting for the Tiger to say, "Good catch!" But he can't say it.

3
All about the Tiger

I don't want you to think that the Tiger is a rotten guy. He's a good guy and a great ballplayer. You definitely want him on your side. He just has this thing about girls. He's not going to get over that.

The Tiger only knows one way to do anything. Once he learns something one way—say, throwing a pitch—that's it. Once he gets to thinking one way—say, about girls—that's it too.

The Tiger throws the ball harder than anyone I know, except the big, tall woodcutter who plays for the Pontiacs, and he's nineteen.

The Tiger throws so hard the ball looks like a marble coming up there, and when he is pitching really good, it is always across the plate—a strike. It is always across the middle of the plate because the Tiger is just grooved to do that. He doesn't throw a curve, or a change-up, or a knuckleball or anything—just a fastball, straight as an arrow, right down the middle of the plate.

So, round about the fourth or fifth inning the hitters start to catch on to this. They start to swing early, and pretty soon they are hitting the Tiger, even though he is lightning fast. The Tiger cannot believe it. He thinks each hit is a fluke, and he won't change it.

There's a grown-up named Art who can show anybody how to throw an "in" or an "out," and how to waste a pitch when you've got them swinging. But for the Tiger there is something not right about this. The Tiger figures he will throw as hard as he can, and you will swing as hard as you can. If you hit it—that's baseball!

What I want to do is to ask Art to show the Tiger how to throw a curveball—in or out, it doesn't matter to me. I know the Tiger won't listen anyway.

I have seen games that the Tiger has lost 2-1,

but if he had dropped down to sidearm once in a while, or even taken some speed off a pitch now and then, they'd be swinging at air and falling out of the box.

The Tiger does not want to be a magician. He wants to be the boss.

Once, last fall, the Tiger and I were playing catch behind the grandstand up at the Ballfield. There was a game going on, and a pretty good crowd watching. But the Tiger could tell that lots of grown-ups were turning around to watch him chuck that ball, whenever the play slowed down.

So the Tiger was really smoking it. When the ball popped into my glove, it sounded like a hammer hitting the fencepost. "Can you handle my fastest?" the Tiger asked.

"Yes, send your best," I said, sitting back on my heels with the glove up in front of my face. I could tell from the Tiger's face between the webbing of my glove, that he wasn't sure, but he let it go anyway. The ball shrank to the size of a pea coming in, right across the heart of the rock we used for a plate. I tried to raise my glove because the ball was rising as it came whistling in, but I wasn't quick enough. The ball hit the top of my glove, ricocheted, and landed—*plonk*—in the middle of my forehead. The lights went out.

I remember thinking, "It was nice of him to ask first." Then I came to, smelling popcorn. Someone had come down from the stands to see if I was OK, and spilled popcorn all over my face.

You'd think the Tiger would want to change his pitch once in a while, but he doesn't. So when the Tiger doesn't say "nice catch!" to a girl, there is no hope that he will.

In the meantime, I will go down to the Cornwallis Café with the Tiger, and be a little bit proud sitting with him in the booth. I will say, "Two orders of chips, please—one gravy, one ketchup." I'll pay this time, he'll pay the next. I will wave to Mei-Ling through the swinging doors of the kitchen, and hold my hand up over my head, the way she does after she catches the ball. She will know I am saying, "Good catch!"

If she smiles back, then I'll know that the next time I need a shortstop, I've got the best. She will play, the Tiger will go on being the Tiger, and we'll have a great team.

Nuts—not just any team but the Ravens!

4
The Tiger Visits Early

Nobody likes getting bad news early, so pardon me. I am still sleeping.

The Tiger is on a tree limb outside my window, and he is tapping on the windowpane.

At first I think it is a tree limb, because the branches overhang my window, but there is no wind this morning. It is still and quiet, and I can see the Tiger with the green hill behind him and the blue sky above. I know what this means, just as surely as I am sleeping here—the Tiger can't make it to the game.

It is almost seven o'clock, a beautiful summer baseball morning. The mist is lifting, and the sunlight will soon swing down the hill to shine through my window. I do not have to get up yet. I am too warm, curled up here in this quilt.

I can hear the sparrows up and quarrelling, but I am going back to sleep.

The Tiger is on the tree limb outside my window. He is tapping on the windowpane, which is already cracked and loose. I have to get up!

I roll back the quilt and get out of bed. The floor is cold. The window goes sliding up and the loose panes wobble in the sash. The Tiger is beaming. He likes being up in the trees and he has news.

"I'm going out on the boat with Danny O'Neill," the Tiger says. He is proud of this, and I wish I'd been asked too. "They've found a bed of scallops off the Island, right in the Basin! We're going out just for the day."

I don't blame the Tiger. This is a good job. Most of the time the boats have to go out for two or three days—or a week, if they are heading down to George's Bank. They don't take kids on those long trips. On a little trip off the Island the Tiger can make twenty bucks a day. I make two bucks a day, some days, carrying bags from the train station to the Long Wharf, when the ferryboat comes in.

Think of the baseballs twenty bucks can buy!

"When are you heading out?" I ask.

"Right now," the Tiger says.

I thought they might be waiting for the tide, but they are leaving from the deep water off the Long Wharf.

"You'll make a few bucks. It's OK."

"I'll miss the game."

"It's a long summer."

"See you when I get back."

"See you."

The Tiger goes down the tree arm over arm, hardly using his legs, except to push himself out from the tree trunk. The Tiger is the only guy I know who can run in a tree! He has proven that in cherry-tree raids. I hear the Tiger thump when he drops to the ground.

I leave the window open. The air smells summer sweet.

I am thinking hard. I need a pitcher! Richard Van Tassel can pitch, if I can get him. OK, I have it figured out. I will put Freddie, our catcher, in to start the game because he has a good arm. I can catch. I'll put Bubby on second base. Whoever I pick up can play first, which is easy. No grounders, anyway—they only have to be able to catch the ball. We are playing Lighthouse Road. That's not so bad. They are a good bunch of ballplayers, and the games we play against them are a lot more friendly than the ones we play against South End.

So this will all work out. I can pick somebody up, even if it's Howard's little brother, Randolph. We can stick him in right field and put Jimmy Christmas on first.

I look around for my clothes. I sleep in my underwear, so I'm OK for underwear. My shirt is on the bedpost, but where are my pants? Geez, I hope Mom didn't wash my pants.

She *did!* I can see them through the window, hanging on the clothesline. How could she wash them when I've got to wear them?

They won't be dry yet. They won't be dry until the sun has been on them a good hour, and the sun is still working its way down the hill behind the house. Well, I can't wait.

I have to find either a first baseman or a right fielder, and I figure I have until about nine o'clock. So I go downstairs in my underwear and shirt, with my sneakers in my hand and a clean pair of socks tucked into them. I walk out into the yard, checking to make sure there is nobody around, up or down the road. The sun feels good on my legs, but my pants are stiff and wet.

I bring my pants in and stuff them into the oven. I throw some shavings and kindling into the stove and open up the drafts to get it going, then turn the drafts down to force heat into the oven. I am going to bake my pants dry.

I hate doing this because every time I do, it makes my pants smell smoky. They are generally still wet when I put them on, but at least they are warm. I tell myself they will dry in the sun.

I have a real inspiration as I leave the house. I am going down to French Street to try to get Desi off their team. I think he will play a game for us. Lighthouse Road won't mind me picking up one player. It's better than no game, I think. Desi has always been friendly—he's tall, and he can catch, which is what you want when you have guys like Ronnie Wong throwing the ball all over the field.

As I head down the road, I think it is a beautiful day for baseball. You can really smell the smoke off my pants, so I slow down a little to give them time to air out.

5
We Lose Big

We're halfway through the game, and it's hopeless.

Lighthouse Road has been at bat for about an hour, and we can't get any of them out. They are just pounding the ball out there.

The sun is high and hot and my clothes are sticky with sweat. My whole team is running around in tight, little circles looking up into the bright sun and getting dizzy.

I have a headache from trying to follow the ball up into the sun, and my mouth feels like a copper penny has melted in it. The catcher's mask is hot and heavy. I am wearing my ballcap backward so the mask will fit over it and there is nothing shading my eyes.

I can't see half the time anyway, because the

sweat keeps popping out in little beads on my forehead and running down the iron bars on my mask, into my eyes. This stings. I've half a mind to ditch the mask, but I don't want to get hit on the head again—so I keep it on.

Freddie is not doing so well, but it's not his fault. He is used to pitching maybe one or two innings. Today we don't have an umpire, so the batters are all waiting for good pitches. Freddie is exhausted by the second inning. Most of the time when he pitches we get a lot of outs off fly balls, but the sun has made every lazy fly ball a three-ring circus.

Most of the time it's not bad playing without an umpire, because you have to get the outs by fielding, and we all get practised up.

Today, with the bright sun and Freddie lobbing them in, Lighthouse Road is really lifting them out there—real rockets. No one can track the ball, and I am afraid that pretty soon someone is going to get conked on the bean.

There hasn't been a ground ball or a line drive for three innings. Mei-Ling and Desi are just standing around.

I call a time-out. Lighthouse Road has provided a big jug of spring water and they are letting us drink out of it. Every inning or so they send two of the little kids off to the spring to fill it up again.

We all have a drink. It is blazing hot. I take a look around.

Lighthouse Road has a beautiful ballfield. It is a meadow on the side of Ben Loman Mountain, all grass, and ditched on the lower end so it's not too wet, even in the spring. By now it has dried out pretty well and the ball gets a good, regular bounce. You could practise infield here. I like a field like this. On smooth grass, you don't get the ball in the mouth on a bad hop, and you don't mind sliding home in a tight game.

This meadow is part way up the mountain, and you can see the fishing boats off in the distance. They look tiny, coming in and going out on the Bay. Today, they are working off Scout Island. That's where the Tiger is.

There is a spruce forest growing up the mountainside at the high end of the ballfield.

We play the low end. It slopes a bit downhill to the road, but not enough to hurt the play. You just think you're batting downhill a bit, and I don't mind that.

They keep two brown cows here to eat the grass and, before we start playing, Brian and David, the Lighthouse Road captains, pull up the steel bars that tether the cows and drag them off to one side of the field so they don't get hit by a wayward ball. These cows are a good idea because they keep the grass low and smooth. The little kids on the home team have to clear off all the cow pies.

I like it here—even today.

The only problem with this field is that by halfway through the game the new ball we got off South End is green from the outfield grass and turning greener every time it hits the ground. Unlike the red dust of our field, these grass stains won't wash off.

I am thinking that maybe we should call this game a loss, rest a bit in the shade and maybe start a new game later. The only problem is I can't remember the score.

"Anybody remember the score?"

"18-6, maybe...."

"No, it's not that high...."

"It doesn't matter. Let's just get a few outs and end the inning."

"We'll make a few changes," I say. "Then we'll go, OK?"

My first move is to bring in Jimmy Christmas as catcher. I am getting out of these shinpads and mask before I pass out.

Then I bring in Bubby to pitch. He has a knuckleball, a real floater.

I put Desi and Mei-Ling, our two best fielders, in the outfield, and bring the other fielders in for a break. That puts Desi, me and Mei-Ling in the outfield. It's a pretty good outfield.

It doesn't really matter if this doesn't work. We are losing anyway. Now we are all set and Bubby takes the mound.

Bubby's knuckleball is a trick pitch. It just floats in there—slow and no spin at all. Sometimes it drops, and sometimes it doesn't. Batters swing themselves off their feet trying to hit it.

Bubby floats the first knuckler in, big as the moon, and Brian, the tall blonde guy with the butch haircut, gives it a high ride. It looks as if it's going to shoot up toward the spruce trees on the mountain, but he doesn't get all of it; he was too far under it. Brian knows it too, from the way he slaps the bat to the ground.

Mei-Ling drifts back, her baseball glove held above her face, shading her eyes as she tracks the ball. Then she turns and runs to a little clump of stunted spruce at the end of the meadow, where she turns again and faces the falling ball. Her arm is up, and it drops—*plop*, into her glove, as if that's where it's meant to go. She hauls it in and throws the ball back to Desi in shallow centre, who chucks it the rest of the way into the infield. One out—a great out! It's a 120-metre drive, and still an out.

"That's the way!"

"Go get 'em, Bubby!"

It is strange how one play can give you heart, and make the game fun again.

Bubby whiffs the next guy on three big pitches. Three knuckleballs that really knuckle.

They come up to the plate, easy—like they are floating down stream; then they drop off the falls. Turnbull is up and Bubby strikes him out. It's the first time this afternoon, and even the Lighthouse Road little kids laugh at this.

Now we've got two outs on four pitches. Soon we will be in the shade, waiting our turn at bat, drinking that cool spring water.

I think the breeze coming down off the mountain is making Bubby's knuckleball drop so well, but I am not pretending to understand knuckleballs.

The next guy up is David's little brother, Joey, who is having the best afternoon of a baseball lifetime. With one foot out in front of the plate, he hits a knuckleball straight up, maybe thirty metres. The ball is up there so long everybody sort of drifts toward it, thinking it is their ball. But this is the catcher's play and Jimmy circles under it. He's got to catch it, otherwise it will hit him. The problem is, Jimmy is wandering around in those little circles, looking up, which means he has lost the ball in the sun.... Better him than me.

Ronnie, who has run in from first base, collides with Jimmy, and I'm concerned now that the ball will either drop on the ground or bounce off someone's ballcap. But just then Desi, who thinks quicker than I do—but not as much—comes charging in. He brushes by Ronnie, reaches up and over Jimmy and catches the ball in a mid-air jump, snaring it just as he goes over the plate. Desi's speed keeps him going until he slips in the grass and sprawls headlong into the drainage ditch.

Desi is not hurt. The ditch is lined with soft earth.

It is the first time I have seen an outfielder catch the ball in front of home plate. It is a marvel. It will be remembered.

With the mountain breeze and Desi's catch, we can ride comfortably on Bubby's knuckleball for the rest of the afternoon. We lose, and we lose big, 31-18, but we get the side out regular. We take our licks.

That trick of Mei-Ling's, with the glove held up against the sun, is something to remember too. I try it and find you can see the ball through the fingers of the glove. No kidding!

"Good game," the Lighthouse Roaders say.

"Good game, we'll get you next time."

"That was some comeback."

"Too late, you guys were too far ahead."

"Too good, you mean."

We all laugh. I think they are happy to beat us—the same as we are happy to beat South End—but I don't mind losing to these guys.

They all smile the same big friendly smile, and they share their water jug. Their meadow field on the side of Ben Loman is worth the walk out from Town.

6
A Swim at the Grill

The game with Lighthouse Road is over and we are walking home. We leave the highway and head down through a clump of tall, pine trees on the edge of a sandy ridge. We are going to the Grill for a swim.

You can smell the hot day there, because of the pine needles. They smell like liniment. Below the ridge there's a little trout stream with a white, sandy bottom. It's full of trout, but they are too small to catch.

This trout stream runs into the sea at a place called the Racket. Before you get to the Racket there's a saw mill and a mountain of sawdust. A little way below the mill there's a small waterfall over some granite boulders, with a deep hole at the bottom, where you can swim.

We call the falls the "Grill."

The falls are only about chest high, and the Grill is actually an iron grill that stops pulp logs heading downstream from going out to sea. There are always a few logs caught there. You can ride them if you want, or make a raft. But on a hot day, it's heads or tails whether you just float in the pool or sit under the waterfall.

I like to sit under the waterfall. It's so cold— like going from the oven to the refrigerator. My headache soon goes away.

When we come here without our bathing suits, we generally don't take off our clothes. After a ball game, we jump in clothes and all.

I take off my sneakers and socks, and tuck what money I have into my ball glove, but I keep my pants on. You can see right through my undershorts when they get wet. Anyway, it will only take a few minutes to get dry again.

The bottom of the pool is so clean you can look down into the water, wiggle your toes in the sand, and see tiny black eels come wriggling out. These eels are as thin as pine needles. I have caught their fathers, out in the deep salt water of the Racket. They have come back from the Sargasso Sea and are as long as a stick and as heavy as a brick.

Freddie is wiggling his toes too, and watching the eels come out of the sand. Except for the two of us, the only ones interested in these little eels are the kingfishers that sit on the pine branches overhanging the pool.

It is pretty funny to see Mei-Ling splashing around the Grill with the guys. I wish the Tiger was here. He probably wouldn't even get into the water.

He would say he didn't feel like swimming.

"Pretty good, eh?" I say to Freddie.

"Lot better than the ball game."

"Yeah ... I'm going to get a drink from the spring."

We don't drink from the same water we swim in: the little kids with us won't walk into the woods to go to the bathroom. So we have a spring up in the pines. We used clam shells to dig down into the sandy earth, and lined the hole with stones.

"Bring me back a drink."

"Have one for me, will ya?"

These are jokes.

Afterward we dry out on the granite slabs from the abandoned railway trestle. The slabs are big enough to stretch out on, and weigh a ton. They used to support the trestle bridge built here so that the big, steam locomotive could cross this hollow. Howard and Jimmy are lying on the slabs, with their baseball gloves as pillows under their heads. Actually both of the gloves they are lying on are Howard's, because Jimmy Christmas hasn't got one. He must have had one once because he is a really good outfielder. Anyway, for every game, Howard, who comes from a big family, brings an extra glove. At the start of every game Howard tosses Jimmy the glove and Jimmy plays with it. At the end of the game Jimmy thanks him and tosses it back. It is kind of a ritual.

Finally, we have to walk the rest of the way home, carrying the heavy canvas bases. Lighthouse Road doesn't have bases, so we take ours out there.

My pants are almost dry, but I have sores on the insides of my legs from this morning, when they were wet, and from swimming in them just now. I will rub the sore places with Vaseline when I get home. As my pants dry, the smoky smell comes back. It follows me like a dog.

There's no game tomorrow, so I'll get my mom to wash my pants with soap. I'll hang around home and wear my shorts if I have to, and let my sores scab over.

7
Jack-knife Baseball

We are playing French Street. We haven't had a game since we lost to Lighthouse Road, and wouldn't you know—it's raining. When the rain begins it seems that it will not go on for very long, so we stand under the trees and wait. The Ballfield drains well, and if the rain lets up a little we can play the game out.

Only it gets worse, and the rain comes down in sheets that sweep across the field toward us. We make a break from the trees to the school-bus shed, where Dougie's father works.

Dougie's dad is surprised to see us, but he lets us in. He has a big box of clean rags from Frenchy's in the corner by the grinding bench, and we use them to dry off and then chuck them back in the box. We are stuck here. The shed has a tin roof and the rain hitting it sounds like drums in a parade.

It is a big shed so they can bring the schoolbuses inside. They've got everything here—tools and equipment for working on the buses—just like a garage. Even though the place is clean and has a cement floor, it smells like oil.

We are all standing around, looking around at the shed, doing nothing. Then Desi takes a jack-knife out of his back pocket. He sits down on a wooden bench by Dougie's dad's toolbox, straddling it as if he was riding a horse.

Desi opens up the blade halfway and sticks the point into the bench. Then, with one finger under the case, he flips the jack-knife up into the air. It lands point down into the bench.

Dougie's dad looks over, but it is only an old bench. This is OK.

"That's a two-base hit," Desi says, "a double."

"He can do that every time," Philippe, Desi's little brother, says.

I sit down opposite Desi. This is a new game for me.

"I don't know how it goes," I say. This makes Desi happy because now he gets to explain the game and show off at the same time.

"You put one finger from your left hand in front of the tip," Desi says, "so the knife can trip over it. And you flip the case up like this...."

Desi goes tip, trip, flip.

"Unless you're left-handed," Bubby says.

Desi nods. He is very easy going. "You get three tries, three outs, same as baseball. A flip is an out if the knife doesn't stick in and stand up."

Desi flips the jack-knife again. It flops over on its side. This is clearly an out.

"Now if it lands like this ..." Desi flips again, and the knife lands on its back, blade up. "... that's a home run!"

The French Street kids laugh. My guess is that Desi can do this whenever he wants.

"This is a single," Desi says, and the blade lands point down, with the case touching the bench. It looks like a teepee.

"A double," Desi continues, and this flip

lands with the blade stuck in the bench and the case hanging in the air. "You have to flip it just a bit harder for a double or a triple. It's a triple when it's bent over, almost on its back."

"No base stealing," Desi say. "Runs on hits only. Let's play."

"How many innings?" I ask. This question puzzles him.

"Well, you play until you don't want to play anymore," he says. "That's the rule."

We start to play, me against Desi.

The French Street kids' eyes light up. Philippe is already laughing, because he knows Desi is a jack-knife wizard.

Because the French Street players are younger and smaller than we are, and we usually beat them at baseball, they are going to enjoy Desi beating me … and they do.

Desi hands me his jack-knife to let me go first.

"Most of the time," he says, "you play with your own knife, because if it lands funny and breaks, it's your knife you broke."

I can understand why this would lead to

arguments; I am grateful he lets me use his knife.

My first time up, I flip the knife off the bench—Out Number 1. The blade clatters along the cement floor. I look at Desi; I am really sorry. Then I flip again and get a single—again, a double. This is pretty good, I think. Next flip the blade doesn't stick in enough and the knife falls over. Out Number 2.

Bubby is pressing in behind my shoulder. He gasps whenever I flip the knife. Everybody is pressing in, trying to see.

"Gimme some room, will ya?"

"You've still got one out left," Bubby says.

I give Bubby a strong "I think I know that" look. I sneak a peek at Desi. He wants me to drive these runners home because he wants me to like the game.

The knife goes up in a nice little twirl, the blade slips down, sticks in the bench, leans over, stays up! It's a … a … a … triple, although it comes this close to being an out!

"Two to nothing," Bubby says. I take the lead.

Desi laughs. The next flip I flip my third out and leave the guy stranded on third base.

Then Desi gives me a lesson. He loads the bases, quickly, one-two-three singles in a row, careful not to hit a double, same little spin, blade coming down with the case.

"Watch this," one of the French Street kids says. They have seen this before.

The knife goes up, flips over three somersaults in the air, and lands flat on its back, blade up. It's a home run! It's 4-2, and nobody out.

All French Street is getting a charge out of this. Desi is smiling too, but not too much because he doesn't want me to quit. I know now this is a joke; a set up. But all I can think of is: how many times did he have to practise this? How many rainy mornings?

I play Desi three more innings. He does stunts like three triples in a row, which is not easy. He throws in a home run to clear the bases whenever the scoring gets complicated. French Street loves this. Desi is their hero. Desi is the king of jack-knife baseball.

"That's it for me," I say. When I think I have served my time.

"Good game," Desi says.

"Yeah, ask me again when you need a patsy."

I get up from the bench, and Desi does too. A little French Street kid sits down quickly, and Bubby takes him on. Why do I know Bubby will lose too? Is it because the little kid sat down so fast?

I decide that as soon as it stops raining I am going home to dig my jack-knife out of the box under my bed. I am going to start practising, and I am going to practise and practise, and not let anybody know that I am even interested in this game—until I am really good.

I will get up an hour earlier every morning, and stick knives in wood, until I am a jack-knife baseball killer. I am going to get so good! I imagine myself blindfolded, playing by sound and touch.

Some rainy day I will ask Desi, would he like a couple of innings of jack-knife, maybe?

I will run up the score on him, flip, flip, flip, and no one will even know I practised—harder than Rocky Colavito hit baseballs.

I tell myself this until I believe it.

I hope to get out of here soon, because the smell of oil is making me sick, and I don't want to throw up in front of the guys.

The rain is quieter now, tapping like fingernails on a kitchen table. I wander over to talk to Dougie's father. His name is Otis, but I call him Mr. Van Tassel. He is working inside an orange schoolbus, ripping out the seats. This is interesting because you can see what holds the seats down.

I am hoping that Otis will drag the Ballfield with his truck. He has done this before. We cut a whole bunch of birchpoles and tie them together like a big, flat broom, and he drags them behind the truck to gather up the stones and rocks.

You have to be careful because if you drag on a wet day the tires leave marks in the field, but if it is too dry the dust chokes you. You have to have a day in between wet and dry. Otis knows the kind of day you need.

When the stones are all at the end of the

field, we get together and throw them down into the drainage ditch. This way you don't have to be afraid of a grounder hitting a stone, and jumping up to hit you in the nose.

This has happened to me so often my mom doesn't stay with me anymore when I get stitched up. She has to get back to The Oaks and I walk home alone holding the cotton batting up to my face. A real ballplayer would go back to the game, I know. But I generally go home and suck ice cubes.

Otis says there is no point in dragging the field this summer, because the Town is going to go to work on it.

"They are going to put the Town workmen to work on it," he says.

"What are they going to do?"

"I don't know. I just heard it."

I thank him for the news, but I don't like it.

The rain has stopped enough for us to leave. The little one has beaten Bubby at jack-knife baseball. I can see from the look in Bubby's eyes that he is telling himself he is going to go home and start practising this stupid game.

We talk about the Ballfield all the way home. Soon everybody drops off at his street, and I am alone and wondering.

And what I am wondering is: who are *they* and what is the *work?*

8
The Ballfield

Our field is up behind the dairy, near the school.
We call it the Ballfield. It doesn't have a name
like Point Pleasant Park or the Wanderer's
Grounds. We just call it the Ballfield.

There is no grass on our field—only hard, red
dirt packed down. The stones work their way
up through. It's a tough field. I like the grass
on Lighthouse Road's meadow, but if you can
play on our field, you can play anywhere. This
is because the ball hits the ground so hard and
comes up so fast, and the hops it takes are so
unreal, that it makes you a good fielder.

Once I was playing shortstop on our field
when the ball came off the bat fast and ugly. It
just skipped along the ground, and I came in to
cut it off with my head down on the ball the

way you're supposed to and with both hands out in front. I squared my chest around thinking it would hit me there, hop off, and I could pick it up and throw the runner out. Instead it took a terrific hop, off the baked brick, and caught me full in the mouth. *Smacko!*

How my lips bled! How funny the blood looked in the red dirt. How funny I looked when the Doc sewed me up, top and bottom. I had big bristles hanging out of my ballooned up lips, and I went home again to suck ice cubes.

We have two dugouts, one on each side of the field—one for each team. They are really just posts stuck in the ground, boarded up on one side and on the roof. They keep out the sun, but they don't keep out the rain.

When you all sit together in the dugout, you are a team. You can talk and figure out what you are going to do. The dugout is where you chuck your glove when you're mad and where you cool off on a hot day.

There are dates and names of teams pencilled or cut into the benches in our dugouts—like on old school desks. There are a thousand scores of old ball games, including games my brother played in. My brother has been in the army—I don't know how long—and his name is there.

People tell me my father was a left-hander on this field. They should have put his name on the bell that hangs outside the Post Office, but he drowned in fresh water. They said that didn't count because all the other names are of people who died at sea. I never saw him play, but he was left-handed, I know, because I've still got his glove. My uncle Teddy told me he pitched for the Ravens when they were a real travelling team.

The only trees are in the outfield, where the Ballfield turns into pastureland. The road is called Old Pit Lane because there's a field for peeling pit props on one side of the Ballfield. This is where the Tiger waits when we have a game. He has to be talked into coming onto the Ballfield.

We have a backstop made out of weir poles and chicken wire. We sweep the stones off the field every spring as soon as the frost is out of the ground, and the spring rains end. Then the ground comes up like hard-baked brick. You could bowl on it, if it weren't for the stones.

The Ballfield is not much of a field, but it is big and open, and level, and you can always smell the warm milk there from the dairy. When you stand in the middle of our field, and someone hits the ball high in the air—into the blue, blue sky—it's as if you are standing in the middle of the biggest ballpark in the world. The blue sky is the same, the ball is the same, and the fear of dropping it is the same fear that has knifed the heart of every waiting fielder since the game began.

You've got to understand how much the Ballfield means to us. If we didn't have a field then French Street couldn't come up here and play us, and then we couldn't go down there and play them.

Like I say, it's our field, and if you can play here, you are prepared. It doesn't get any harder, and every other ballpark is just a bag of toys.

9
Lost Ball

South End cannot understand how we can beat them and then lose to Lighthouse Road. I tell them, "We only get up for the big games."

South End hasn't been around very much lately. They have a van and they have been playing the teams from the towns up the Valley. They are pretty lucky—having a van with seats in it. We are playing French Street and Lighthouse Road a lot. We've got a game lined up with Marshalltown and if we can get a ride out, we got a game with Indian Hill.

Today we are playing French Street down on the Cannonbanks. The Cannonbanks is a field near the beach, mostly grass and fine shale. It's a safe field to play on, but you have to be careful because there is a small slope running along the right side of the field, and if the ball gets by the right fielder it will run down the slope and into the tide water. Everybody knows not to hit the ball too far to right field.

Buttments built of logs and stones keep the banks from slipping into the Bay. There are old cast iron cannons lining the field overlooking the harbour so you keep your head up, going for fly balls, so you don't run into a cannon.

Another problem with the Cannonbanks is a long, low bingo hall on the left side of the ballfield. Hit the ball over the top of the hall and you've got a home run. Hit it off the roof and you've got a double. Hit the side of the building and you've got trouble—a broken window.

The Tiger is back and he's pitching for us. This is OK by me, but a lot of the French Street kids can't get around his fastball, which is all the Tiger has. They are swinging late and if they connect, the ball flies off to the right side toward the Bay.

Already Bubby has had to scramble down

the Banks a dozen times to pick up the ball from among the stones on the seashore. And once, both teams had to hunt for the ball among the stones in the cribwork of the buttments. Today we only have the one good ball. Desi, the big gun for French Street, is at bat and I know the Tiger is going to try to strike him out.

"Let him hit," I say to the Tiger, but the Tiger won't back off. He chucks it in there. Strike one. Desi digs in, the bat twitching over his shoulder. The Tiger chucks, Desi nicks it, and the ball bounces down and comes off Freddie's ankle. We have a five-minute wait while Freddie hops around. The Tiger is over behind the mound, laughing into his glove.

After everybody has calmed down, the Tiger winds up to throw it in there, and Desi connects hard, but a little late because of the Tiger's speed. The ball screams off toward right field and the water of the Bay. We all run toward the edge of the Cannonbanks, because if you see it land, you've got a chance.

"You should've let him hit it square," I say to the Tiger.

He gives me a funny look.

We get to the edge of the Banks just in time to see the ball splash into the water. We scramble down hoping that the tide will swing the ball into shore. No ball, no game.

The tide swings the ball out from shore. It is strange to see the ball floating up and down on the waves. The little breeze blowing onshore is not strong enough to push the ball against the tide.

"It's heading toward the Long Wharf," Mei-Ling says.

We tear off along the path beside the Cannonbanks that leads to the Long Wharf, dropping equipment as we go. The run quickly becomes a race, and it is interesting to see, as we pelt along, who can run and who can't.

The Tiger can run. He is thick and strong through the middle, but he can't run as fast as Mei-Ling. Mei-Ling runs like a deer. I go up on my toes, pretending I am a horse, and pass the Tiger. I look back and see that he has slowed to a walk. If the Tiger is not the best at something, he doesn't do it.

"There it is," I say. The ball is bobbing up and down on the waves sloshing under the wharf. Down we go. Sunlight streaming through the cracks between the planks makes ripples of light in the green water. Little blue periwinkles and fat white barnacles hang in the seaweed on the pilings.

I have lost sight of the ball. So has everyone else. We fan out, crawling on the lattice work of the wharf's timbers, in among the pigeon nests, looking for the ball in the green water below.

"There it is," somebody says, but I can't see who it is. I crawl over to where the kid is hanging off the cribwork around one of the wharf pilings, but it is not the ball he sees in the water; it is just a round stone covered with white barnacles, half out of the water.

It is kind of spooky down here, like a cave, but I like it. When Freddie steals a cigar from his father, this is where we come to smoke it. I have been sick here at least twice.

Nobody can see you down here underneath the wharf, but you can look up through the cracks between the planks and see the fishermen walking along in their big boots. You can hear everything they say. You can be this close to them and they can't see you. You can sit under here when they are sitting on the wharf, talking about their catch, what they dragged, and where they got it. They brag about taking half a tonne of cod in one drag, and they don't know you are listening. They say everything as if there isn't a kid around. The wharf planks above your head bump and rumble when a truck goes over. The pigeons fly in and out to their nests, flapping their wings, and their droppings go into the water in long, white ribbons.

In the spring, when the pigeons have their chicks, you can crawl right up the slimy plank to the cross pieces where the pigeons build their nests. They won't move if they have a chick in their nests, but you can't touch the chicks or the mother won't come back. This is a fact.

Bubby took a chick from its nest and raised it on milk and crackers. When the baby-blue feathers turned to gun-metal blue, Bubby flew the grown-up bird from a string over the Cannonbanks until Constable Connolly, who is the police officer for the ferry terminal, told him to let it go. Bubby says it flew right back to the exact same spot he took it from. I believe it.

I would never take a pigeon from the wharf pilings, and I hate smoking, but I often come down here to pick off the periwinkles. If you can find an apple-juice tin on the beach you can boil up the periwinkles and eat them with a hairpin. I get the hairpins from my sister. They are good for getting the periwinkles out of the shells.

"There it is!" This yell interrupts my thoughts.

Dougie Van Tassel has spotted the ball. We run toward his voice, somewhere off in the rippling darkness of the wharf pilings.

"Can't reach it, though. Too deep there."

The ball is at the very end of the wharf, where the ferry comes in. It is bobbing up and down, and going around and around a piling in an eddy—like a ride on a carousel.

We watch it go round the post a few times. Then Mei-Ling, who is the tallest, at least in the legs, begins to wade out. I shudder. This is deep and cold salt water. Everybody knows this is where the sharks come in, because this is where the ferryboat throws all its garbage. I have never seen a shark here, but everybody knows they are here, under the water.

I have seen flatfish sliding around the posts and pilings, and you can catch yourself a crab here anytime, just by dropping in a bit of bacon tied on a string. You don't even need a hook— the crab won't let go of the bacon. So I am not particularly crazy about wading around here.

Mei-Ling can't reach the ball; she is up to her waist already and she is not even halfway there. I am sure that the Tiger has never done this before, but he and I and everybody else who has ever seen a Tarzan movie knows what we have to do.

The Tiger wades in and he takes Mei-Ling's hand. Mei-Ling is calm and quiet, but the Tiger is splashing around a lot with his free hand. I know what he is doing—he is scaring the sharks. He hasn't seen any, either, but we both know they are there.

I wade in and take the Tiger's free hand. Mei-Ling wades out a few more feet. She is up to her chest now, and there is still a long way to go. Desi wades in; he is the anchor. He is the biggest of us, and the strongest except for the Tiger. We will never know which one is the strongest because they won't arm wrestle. If one of them lost—which one of them would—we could never play ball together again.

Now Mei-Ling is in over her head. I know this for a fact, because she is floating in the tide, just like the ball. Finally, Mei-Ling nabs the ball—*swish* it goes, *splash*, into her hands. She looks back and smiles. The Tiger smiles. He has her strong in his grip, hand-to-hand—no problem.

Desi pulls us back in. We scramble up the stones and cribwork. I am numb from the waist down. This is cold salt water! I've got to get into the sun. The Tiger is embarrassed. I sneak a look at Mei-Ling. Her wet T-shirt is sticking to her skin and you can see right

through it; but she is smiling. We climb back up the wharf into the sunshine. It feels great. We've got the ball!

The Tiger does not speak. The French kids are talking a mile a minute. They think this is the greatest thing ever, bar none.

"Let's go to the Grill," Desi says.

"Good idea."

We call the game a draw. This does not go down well with the Tiger because he has two dimes in his back pocket, meaning twenty wins for the season, which is hall of fame stuff if you can keep it up. We were ahead in the game. I agree to call it a draw, because the ball is too wet to play with.

"They could have come back," I tell the Tiger.

We are a funny parade walking along Water Street to the Grill. Our clothes are wet, we are covered with sand, there are oil stains on our T-shirts, and we are carrying all our ball gear—two bats, gloves, a pitcher's mask, and bases.

The Tiger is walking with Mei-Ling. They flip the ball back and forth between them, as if it were a new toy.

10
Mei-Ling at the Ell

There is no milk for breakfast, so I am walking in the early morning chill, to the corner store for milk. Going past the school I see Mei-Ling with an India rubber ball. She is in the Ell, where the new wing has been built onto the school. I see her but she doesn't see me.

An India rubber ball is not like an ordinary sponge rubber ball. It's harder, for one thing. You can't play stinger-miss with it, for sure. An India rubber ball bounces higher on the second bounce, and still higher on the third. So you can't miss it or you'll lose it. Bubby Neville had a ball like this and he lost it bouncing it downhill on Birch Street. He told me when it crossed the tracks it was bouncing over the telephone lines. I believe it. So this India rubber ball she is throwing is a live-wire thing to play with.

Mei-Ling is bouncing the India rubber ball against the brick wall of the school so it will hit the ground first and then rebound up in the air. The ball goes up sharp. She drifts back, her glove hand held above her forehead, tracking the ball against the sun. So that's where that magic trick came from.

When the ball comes down, she catches it with two hands so it can't pop out. She whirls to her left, plants her left foot, whips her arm around and throws one long, straight clothesline to the other wall forming the Ell. It's as if she's playing shortstop and throwing to first base.

Because this throw hits the wall first, the ball rebounds low and comes back to Mei-Ling as a grounder. She squares to the ball, scoops it up, and begins the same play again … and again. If you've ever wanted to know how to pick up a grounder backhanded, you should be here now.

I have thrown a ball against a brick wall for

hours. I have thrown stones against a steel garage to hear it ring, and I have thrown stones all afternoon at a floating tin can until it either sank or floated out of sight. But I have never seen anybody do this. This is like pop flies and grounders, over and over.

I wonder why she is doing this, because she is already the best fielder we have. What Mei-Ling is doing is more like dancing than baseball.

Long after I get home with the milk, after I have spent the afternoon carrying bags for the tourists from the ferry dock to the train station, and even after I have had my rhubarb grunt, chucked my shirt on the bedpost, and gotten into bed, I am still wondering why she would do that. How many kinds of balls did she try before she found out that an India rubber ball was perfect for this kind of practice? How many early mornings does she do this before going off to the Café to cut vegetables?

I am half asleep when the answer comes. Not even remembering that I was still trying to think of an answer, I know what it is. She wants to be as good as the Tiger.

11
Sodding the Field

I am sloshing through the kite field by Old Pit Lane, about seven o'clock in the morning. The grass and burdocks are still wet from dew. After a few minutes in the wet grass it is just like wading in the shallows. I knew it would be like this, so I've got my rubber boots on.

I am on my way to the Ballfield. They have been stripping the bark off pit props and pulp logs here this past two weeks, and the smell of rotting bark is pretty strong—sweet, like burnt sugar. When it rots it can be pretty gooey, but the top layer is just damp from the rain. The dry stuff underneath crunches under my boots. As I come across the pit prop field, I can see a truck down by the Ballfield.

It's true! Dougie's father, Otis, told Dougie

and Dougie told me that the Town gave Mr. Budd a contract for sod.

It's hard to believe! They are going to sod the Ballfield.

Budd's old green flatbed is piled with sod, good grass turf, cut into long strips and rolled up like a carpet. Mr. Budd is in the cab smoking a cigarette, waiting for the Town men to show up. Smoke is curling out of the cab window. Budd cuts it, and delivers it, but the Town has to lay it. Budd's back is not so good.

Mr. Budd is good at waiting, and he smiles when he sees me coming. His boy, James, and my brother, Wink, went into the army together. Wink's still there, I hope—though we haven't heard from him lately.

"Nicky," Mr. Budd says, "I got an outfield here."

I look at the sod on the flatbed. It is all rolled up like jellyrolls, but I can imagine it spread out and covering the red dirt of the whole outfield. This green grass will look great against the red-dirt infield. I like red and green. Geez, it's just like Christmas!

You don't grass the infield, but maybe they will put a couple of loads of clay on it. That would be great. That would be heaven on earth.

"Town's going to fix up the backstop too," Mr. Budd says, "so's the ball won't run down the hill."

Tell me about it. I have watched the Pontiacs hit foul balls over the backstop, and seen them bounce off a windshield, land in the ditch, roll into a culvert and disappear down a storm drain. Goodbye two bucks.

"What about the infield?" I say hopefully to Budd.

"Not in the contract," Budd says. "But that's not too hard; maybe two loads of good, clean clay. You get some guys to spread it out."

My mind is working fast—not well, but fast. I am thinking I can get Desi and French Street to help us Ravens. We could do it in a day. If Budd will dump the clay around the bases, we could spread it out.

There's a big concrete roller down by the Manor, which is a boarding house now but used to be a hotel—with tennis courts. The courts are all covered in grass and weeds, but I have seen the roller there a hundred times; no one ever uses it. This will work!

"I can get some guys," I say to Budd. "What's the news with James?"

"Fine, doing fine," Budd says. I nod my head. I don't really care how James is doing; he is with Wink, wherever he is. I just want to make sure we get the clay for the infield. I smile at Mr. Budd and he can tell I really want that clay. I hope he's not joking. I think he means it.

I ask Mr. Budd to phone my mom out at The Oaks when he can bring the clay. Two guys from the Town show up to lay the sod, so I go off to hunt up the Tiger, and Bubby maybe— anybody really. It would be great if I could find the Tiger, but I really just want to tell somebody the news. Boy, I can't wait to see their faces!

I am running up through the pit-prop field when I trip. Down I go into the warm, crunchy, sweet-smelling bark. The bark shavings stick to my clothes as if I had been sprayed with glue!

12
The Tiger Learns How

It is always good to meet up with the Tiger, but right now I am anxious to tell him about the outfield grass.

I catch up with him down on Main Street, where he is standing with Walter the Umpire just outside the plate glass window of *The Weekly Thunder* building. Walter is giving the Tiger one of his famous lectures. I hate these lectures—particularly when I've got real news to tell.

Walter is a tall, thin typesetter in the print shop and he is all dressed up to go to work. He is a very tidy guy, in a white shirt and corduroy pants, and a big blue bow-tie. Over it all he is wearing a long white apron, like a cook's, to keep the ink off his clothes. These white clothes make him look like a stork.

It is too good to be true. Right there in the street Walter is telling the Tiger how to throw a curveball. Why, he will show him how right now. Walt has a baseball in his long, piano-playing fingers. The ball has black, electrical tape on it, so I recognize it as the Tiger's. It's always a mistake to walk past Walt with a baseball in your hand if you're in a hurry.

"Now," Walt says, "you put two fingers across the seams, like this, and on the bottom …" He flips the ball over so you can see his hold on the bottom. "… your thumb and pinkie go here."

Walter is a grown-up for sure, because he has certainly stopped growing—but you can talk to him, no problem. It does not matter whether he is umping our game or the Pontiacs', he umps the exact same way. Often on a Saturday he will ump our game in the morning and the Pontiacs' in the evening.

People say that back at his place on Maiden Lane, where he lives with his mother, he has a box under his bed with a hundred baseballs in it. I believe it.

Walt has the whole outfit for a game: black

umpire shoes, black pants, shin protectors, just like a catcher's, a chest protector that he wears inside his black suit jacket, and a little black umpire's cap with a tiny bill so it won't get in the way of the steel mask. He even has the little clicker that you hold in your hand to keep track of the balls, strikes, and outs. He has the rulebook too, in his back pocket.

Walt has red hair and whiskers. He is thin and long, and his eyes are funny—maybe from umping so much. They are like owl's eyes. He can look two ways at once.

He can be very scary, even though you know he is harmless. You can hit a ground ball to third base, and as you're running to first, you'll see Walt's long legs kicking and his thin arms pumping, and by the time you reach the base, Walt is saying, "Yer out!" He is kind enough to wait until you get there.

He points with a long, bony finger to your foot beside the bag, and that is all the proof anybody needs. Don't bother to argue—he saw the play.

Then he walks slowly back to home plate as

if he's going a funeral. Walt is the only guy I ever saw who umpires home plate and first base at the same time.

I can see that Walt is going to tie us up for a long time with this curveball demonstration. I can't decide what's more important—my news or Walt's lecture. But I can't see any way of breaking into it, anyway.

"Now," Walt says to the Tiger and nods to me, "Van Lingle Mungo held the curve like this...." Walt twists his wrist, holding the ball out so we can see it. "He came across the chest with it like this...."

Walt is well into it now. When he mentions dead guys like Mungo, his voice drops low as if he is praying, and when he gives instructions, his voice gets louder as if he is preaching.

Now Walt's left foot is high in the air, hovering over the Tiger's head. The ball is in his right hand, which is tucked behind his neck. Walt pauses, posing like a statue, and looks down under his armpit at the Tiger to make sure he is paying attention. Mrs. Whatsall taps on the window.

Mrs. Whatsall runs *The Weekly Thunder*, and even though we can't hear what she is saying on the other side of the window, it does not look good. Walt's position sort of collapses, and he says, "Sorry, boys." He has to go back to work.

"Hey," the Tiger says, because Walt has pocketed his baseball. "My ball."

"Ah!" Walt says, as if you struck him.

He flips the ball to the Tiger, and the last we see of him he is hustling down the long hall past the big Heidelburg which cranks out *The Weekly Thunder*.

"Have I got news!" I say, and tell the Tiger all about Mr. Budd and the outfield grass and the possibility of dry clay for the infield. He does not believe me.

"Cross my heart and hope to die," I say.

This oath is not strong enough for the Tiger. I have to swear another, which is secret and so strong I can't say it out loud. If I do, we will both go blind. I say the oath in my head, and nod to the Tiger that I have said it. The Tiger brightens up.

"We'll need rakes," he says. "It will have to be spread on a dry day—the first dry day we get. The rain will be good for the grass but if the clay gets wet we will never get it smoothed out."

"Desi will give us a hand."

"We can count on Ronnie and Mei-Ling," the Tiger says. This surprises me a little.

"I know where we can get a roller," I say. The Tiger looks at me as if I were a genius. We both know where the roller is.

I don't know why we just don't go and ask for it, right then and there. It has been lying in the grass for ten years. But it seems as if the only way we can get it is to go and hook it. That means we have to do it at night, but first we need a plan.

We go up to the Cornwallis Café for chips, and there, in the privacy of the booth, we start making plans. First we check to make sure that there's nobody in the booth next to us.

There is nobody in the next booth. We decide to hook the roller this very night.

13
Ramble in the Brambles

I am accustomed to the wind sweeping the tree branch across my bedroom window. In the winter, when the trees are bare, the branches make a tapping sound. In the summer, when the leaves are out, it is as if someone were sweeping a broom across my window. I can sleep right through all of this. The Tiger knows it, so he stops tapping and opens the window with the loose pane.

I did not mean to fall asleep at all. I still have my clothes on, including my sneakers, and my baseball cap is in my hand.

The Tiger whispers my name. Still it sounds like the wind, and I keep on sleeping.

"Nicky Come-Play-Ball," the Tiger calls again.

I wake up when I hear the Tiger call my nickname, because I am never late for a ball game. The glass rattles in the window. I have not the faintest idea what time it is, but it is dark.

"Let's go, Nick! They're all waiting!"

"I'm ready ... I wasn't sure you were coming."

I look out of my bedroom window. The moon has risen over the hill, and in the shadows of the branches I can see Mei-Ling and Desi, Freddie and Bubby, a shrimp I take to be Desi's little brother, Philippe, and Ronnie.

The moon gives a silver light to the grass and fields. As we climb out of my window onto the branch—the Tiger first, me second—I wonder whether it will hold us both. The branch sags ... creaks, and the Tiger laughs. He must have heard me suck in my breath.

"Big Cat," I say, which is what I call the Tiger when I get anxious. "Get a move on."

The Tiger is enjoying being up in the tree

with Desi and Mei-Ling and the rest watching us. I would just as soon be on the ground. The branch goes up and down, and I know the Tiger is bouncing as if he's on a trampoline.

"Cut it out! My mom will hear us for sure." Sometimes the Tiger is not too bright. He laughs again, and we reach the trunk of the tree. From there it is just like stepping down stairs—going down from one branch to the next, like on a spiral staircase.

We reach the last branch of the oak. The Tiger swings down to the ground, landing firmly on his feet. I do the same thing, only I tumble when I land.

"Dougie won't be here," Bubby says. "He got caught. He was just going out when his father came in."

"Did his father say anything to him?"

"No," Bubby says, " He just got sent back in. I saw the light come on in his bedroom."

"Not everybody's got an oak tree outside their window," I say.

We split up into two groups. In case one group gets caught, the other will continue the mission. I can't imagine anyone looking for us, except my mom—on account of the Tiger being so loud.

Desi takes one group, with Philippe, Freddie and Bubby. Ronnie, Mei-Ling and I head out with the Tiger. Desi starts off down the Lane in a kind of dog trot, so we hustle along too. To shake off pursuers, the Tiger leads us off the beaten path where we wander into a blackberry bramble patch and get scratched and ripped by the prickles. When we finally reach the street, Desi is nowhere in sight.

The streetlights are on, and with the moonlight, we can see everything clearly. Even though the streets are empty, I am deathly afraid of being seen by somebody who knows my mom.

"Did you have to wear those?" I say to the Tiger. He is wearing shoes that have little steel clickers on the toes and heels. He sounds like a pony clopping along the sidewalk. His mother puts the clickers on his shoes to make them last longer.

"Geez, you sound like a tap dancer," I say.

The Tiger knows I am just trying to get even with him for scaring the living daylights out of me by bouncing up and down on the branch outside my window.

The Tiger walks in the shadows on the edge of the lawns. We stick close together. The lilacs are in bloom, and their flowers scrape against my face. I hope I am not going to smell like my sister.

The Tiger is a good leader. We are zigzagging down alleyways and cutting across yards, but I know we are heading for the old tennis courts and the cement roller.

"C'mon," the Tiger says, and I realize that he wants to get there first, ahead of Desi.

We come to a picket fence and the Tiger takes it like a horse going over a jump, touching just one foot on a post as he goes over. Mei-Ling opens the gate and we walk through, Ronnie following behind.

We cut through the graveyard, which does not bother me, although there are strange shapes lurking in the dark. Everybody knows Weird Willie hangs out here after dark, and there are little brown bats swinging around the light by the caretaker's hut, looking for moths. We hurry out through the iron fence on the far side. You get through a graveyard quicker if you keep your eyes shut—I can tell you that.

"How many dead people in that graveyard?" I ask Ronnie.

Puffing like a whale, Ronnie says, "All of them." That is not a joke but more like a grace that you say after you've got through safely.

Now we can see the Manor, and I am relieved that the trees where the tennis courts used to be are in full leaf, because they shade the spot where the roller is stashed. Also, Mrs. Jennings has left her wash on the clothesline, figuring it isn't going to rain. We can walk between the lines of washing without being seen, even if they are looking out of the windows of the boarding house, drunk or sober, in the middle of the night.

"Rats," the Tiger says. "Rats, rats, rats."

I wonder why the Tiger is upset. When I come up beside him, I see Desi and his little

brother, Bubby and Freddie too, sitting in a line inside the boarding-house fence. They are down on their heels in the shadows, like a bunch of crows on a telephone wire, waiting for us to show up. The Tiger gives us all a disgusted look, as though we were responsible for slowing him down.

Suddenly the back door of the boarding house opens. The light from the back porch jumps across the lawn, and there is Mrs. Jennings looking at Desi and the boys, who are caught in the spotlight.

I can't decide whether to run or stand still. I guess I stand still. I'm certainly not running.

Good grief!

14
Mrs. Jennings Cleans House

It is strange how clearly you hear things at night. Hiding in the bushes across the street from the boarding house, we can hear the wind rustling the leaves around us. We can even hear the dreadful silence of Mrs. Jennings as she stares out of her back door at Desi and the boys, lined up on their heels inside her board fence.

I am expecting Mrs. Jennings to come storming out onto her back porch, broom in hand. My thoughts even run to shotguns and rock salt, which Mrs. Jennings has got, I know. She is entirely capable of using them, but instead she slowly steps backward through the kitchen door.

We look at each other in amazement. A retreat

is not what we expected.

"I know she saw Desi. She looked straight at him," the Tiger says.

"She's gone to get the shotgun," I say, "the same one she cut loose on Hallowe'en."

"She loads shells with pepper," the Tiger says.

"No, it was rock salt," Ronnie says. "I was there. You could smell it."

I believe him.

The Tiger is all set to run across the street and drag Desi out of Mrs. Jennings's yard when the porch door opens again, and the light from the kitchen jumps across the lawn like a searchlight pointing at Desi and the boys. They have all stood up by now.

And then we hear—oh so clearly—the unholy rattle of a dog chain. Without anyone saying anything—it is like mind-reading—we all know at the same time that Mrs. Jennings has unleashed the biggest, most awful dog that ever snapped a rat's neck.

Holy liftin'!

Desi has heard the chain rattle too, because

he has grabbed his little brother, Philippe, and is stuffing him over the fence. Better to climb than run!

I do not see the dog, but I know he is heavy because I can hear his footsteps coming off Mrs. Jennings's porch steps.

"Go get 'em, Buck!" she says, in a high, shrill voice that reminds me of the Town fire whistle.

Buck! What a name for a dog! It's a killer! Buck! I mean, what a name for a dog! And that chain rattle means only one thing ... she has let him loose!

"Go get 'em!" she says. "Go get 'em, Buck!"

Mrs. Jennings is out for blood, and it is every guy and girl for themselves. When I take off, Ronnie has already left the scene. Desi has dropped Philippe over the board fence and is scrambling over himself. I can see the Tiger. He is running in the wrong direction, straight toward Mrs. Jennings! Perhaps he is going to help Desi. Mei-Ling, don't ask me why, isn't running at all!

Bubby and Freddie have disappeared among the wash on the clothesline, probably figuring to squeeze through the old iron fence on the far side.

"They will never make it," I am thinking, but that is their problem. They should have climbed.

Everybody knows that when you are being chased by a killer dog you have to climb. It's the same with bears—the dog can outrun you.

Mrs. Jennings's yard is cleaned out in two seconds flat, and there are kids heading off in every direction.

I remember once seeing a red-tailed hawk in full flight hit, *smacko*, an alder bush full of sparrows. The sparrows took off, forgetting they were a flock, leaping into the air, up, down and sideways. This is what Buck and the yard full of kids are like.

I am pretty sure this dog, Buck, is a silent killer because I have not heard him bark. This is bad news, because if a dog has somebody treed, he barks. Right? But if the dog is standing over you, drooling on your face and getting ready to rip out all your soft spots he is not barking, is he?

I can't stop myself from running now.... When I do stop, I have passed Ronnie, and I have no idea where the Tiger or Mei-Ling is. I shudder to think of what has happened to Freddie and Bubby.

Bubby is the slowest. Geez, the dog has probably got him by now. This dog, Buck, which Mrs. Jennings has trained to terrorize, most likely has Bubby by the leg at this moment, dragging him backward toward the house. Mrs. Jennings has probably taught him to do this at the command of a silent dog whistle. This dog is a trained, silent killer! I am going to need a new first baseman!

I decide to head for downtown. This is risky in itself, because there is a nine-o'clock whistle, which means all kids have to be off the street by nine. It is past midnight now, I think. Geez, it must be almost morning! If I can make it downtown I can hide out behind the Cornwallis Café. You go up the back stairs to get to Mei-Ling's apartment. Maybe Mei-Ling and Ronnie will know what has happened to Bubby and Freddie.

The walk calms me down. The streets are empty, and now a soft rain starts to fall. People are turning out the lights in their houses, like candles being snuffed out. Maybe it is not as late as I thought.

When I get to the Cornwallis I crouch down inside the wooden staircase leading up to the second floor. This is where they store the garbage from the Café. It doesn't smell very good here, but at least I am safe.

I open up the wooden garbage bin, which is empty except for one wooden crate used for storing lettuces. I get in and sit on the lettuce crate and let the bin cover down. I hope this is not mouse mealtime, but I am certainly safe here, and the smell of the garbage will cover my scent. The bottom of the bin is greasy and slippery, but it's better than being up against a trained, silent killer dog named Buck. I say a prayer. It's too late for Bubby, I know, but I figure God can do anything He wants, even turn back time.

"Oh, God," I say, picturing Him in my mind like Father Rossignol, who I met setting up pins in the bowling alley under the Catholic church, "do not let that dog, Buck, track me here. If he does get hold of Bubby, let him remember to cover up his soft spots. At least let the brute only rip up his left hand, as he throws with his right. Amen. P.S. If you get me out of this one, God, I absolutely, promise *never* to steal anything ever again, big or small, not even a candy at Haddie's...."

Maybe I did fall asleep for a while. It is the clickers on the bottom of the Tiger's shoes that wake me up. Mei-Ling and the Tiger have collected Ronnie. They are coming down the drive to the Cornwallis, where the food trucks back up, and I can hear the Tiger's shoes clicking like crickets on the pavement, mixed in with Mei-Ling's laughter.

I pop out of the garbage bin. This gets the surprise I am expecting. Desi and his bunch are not here, and neither are Bubby and Freddie. I do not understand why Mei-Ling is laughing.

"No dog," Mei-Ling says. "She just came out rattling a chain."

"And calling, 'Buck, Buck,'" says the Tiger.

"Mrs. Jennings doesn't even have a dog," Ronnie says. "She keeps cats." When the Tiger laughs it is like a bear woofing in the apple orchard. The Tiger is woofing now.

"Bubby? Freddie?" I ask.

"Never came back," the Tiger says.

"Desi?"

"Carrying his brother home by now."

I think about this for a while. We talk a bit about the roller. We decide to go to bed and meet in the morning. We split.

Even though I realize now that Mrs. Jennings does not have a dog, I am so shaken up by her trick that I watch all the long, lonely walk home for a trained, silent killer named Buck … Buck ready to leap out from behind every lilac bush; Buck in every shadow. I do not relax until I have shinnied up the trunk of the oak tree, climbed along the branch to my window, and slipped back inside my bedroom.

Dogs cannot climb trees.

15
The Long, Long Lawn

My room has a sickeningly sweet smell of wet grass and garbage. It is coming off my clothes.

When I wake up, my mom and my sister have already left for The Oaks, where my mom is chief housekeeper. My sister spends the day there too, pressing linen tablecloths and cotton sheets. My mom got her the job.

I am lying here in bed, not wanting to get up at all, when a big, buzzing bluebottle fly comes in through the open window and starts drawing endless circles around my room. Like a fish caught in a weir, he just goes round and round, and can't find his way out. The buzzing grows fainter when he is in the far corners and louder when he zooms over my head. Every once in a while the fly lands, and I think, "Oh no, where is he?" I stick my head out from under the pillow, the fly takes off, and those endless circles begin again.

This is enough to drive anybody nuts or, in my case, to drive me out of bed. I get up and herd the fly out of the window, where he disappears into a beautiful, warm summer day.

The robins are on the lawn outside listening for worms. In the fields away off, the cows are moving slowly down to the ponds. That is the good thing about living on the edge of town— go out and you're out in the country, go in and you're in town.

I decide to go down to Mrs. Jennings and ask for the roller. I need that roller. Got to have it. It's no good getting the clay for the infield unless we can spread, rake, and roll it, or the bumps will be worse than they were before. I hunt through my drawers. I have a clean shirt and some clean underwear, but I have to wear the same socks, and I've only got one pair of pants.

You would think that with two experts in laundry we would have some clean clothes around here. I am a little grumpy until I have my cereal, but after that I cheer up and head down in good spirits to see Mrs. Jennings.

On the way I meet up with Bubby and tell him there was no killer dog. Bubby comes along, mainly to find out if it's true about the dog, but I have a hunch that he will not come right up to the door with me.

Sure enough, when we get there, Bubby hangs back. He wants to see who greets me, Mrs. Jennings or Buck. I am fairly confident that there is no dog, but I am still scared. I don't mind talking to grown-ups, when I absolutely have to, and there is only one thing to do: ask for the roller straight out. I decide to keep telling her I'm sorry until she believes me, and let her know I am considering going to Sunday school. I know she is a strong church-goer.

I decide to knock on the front door—much grander than the porch door, which Mrs. Jennings came out of last night.

This boarding house used to be a summer hotel for tourists. There is a fine entrance, with marble steps like gravestones, leading up to the door, which has a big pane of frosted glass. Even though it's frosted, I can see inside and get a look at who's coming.

I look over my shoulder and see Bubby strolling along, as if he just happens to be walking by here, on the way to somewhere else.

I hear footsteps coming down the hallway. Little thumps. There's no dog.

The big glass door opens and Mrs. Jennings pushes the screen door back. A cat curls up around her legs.

"Oh, Fluffy!" Mrs. Jennings says. "Go away." She gives Fluffy a little push with her foot.

"Yes?" she says to me.

"Good morning," I say, but I don't know whether to call her Mrs. or Miss. What do you call a widow?

I am stuck already. I am afraid I am going to blush. I blush.

"Ma'am," I say. *Good, I got out of that one.*

"Yes?" she says, and she nods as if to say, "OK, you can begin anytime you like."

Mrs. Jennings has a funny cast to her right eye, as if it is drifting off on its own. I try not to stare. Then, I am not sure why, I spill my guts.

"I was one of the kids in your yard last night," I say. "We were trying to steal that old roller you have out back. We wanted to roll the Ballfield."

"Well," Mrs. Jennings says, "I didn't think you wanted the wash."

"If there's a mess," I say, "I'm here to clean it up." Then I have an inspiration. "Me—and my friend there," I say, and I point over my shoulder to Bubby, who is walking by for his second or third circuit of the sidewalk across the street.

"Young man!" Mrs. Jennings shouts to Bubby. "Young man, come over here. I've got something for you to do!"

Bubby gives me one dirty look—"enemies for life"—but he comes over. He's wearing his baseball cap with the Orioles' bird on it. He always wears it, and now he takes it off as he walks across the street, holding it out in front of him.

This is surrender.

"Come with me, boys," says Mrs. Jennings, and she leads us into the house, which is very cool and grand, with long runners down the hallways and up the stairs, and plants in big pots, and a cat on every sofa.

We are halfway down the hallway when Mrs. Jennings suddenly swivels around, looks straight at Bubby, cocks her cast eye at me, and says sharply, "Not afraid of dogs, are you?"

We do not answer. She laughs. I don't know whether she is kidding or not, but I am very relieved to get to the other end of the house with no Buck in sight.

We come out of the kitchen and onto the back porch. Mrs. Jennings wrestles an old hand mower out of her garden shed.

"You do the lawn," she says, "and you can have the roller."

I look at Bubby and then at the lawn, and it is hard to tell which is longer, Bubby's face or the grass.

"We can do it, Bubby," I say. "We start now, we can finish by noon."

We realize that we have to rake up the clippings too—this is a lot of work. So Bubby goes down to French Street to fetch Desi and Philippe, while I start mowing.

In the end it is not so bad, because when Desi and his kid brother come up, we sling a rope around the mower and pull it two at a time, like oxen pulling a load of logs out of the woods. One of us steadies the handle.

The day is hot and sunny. The little green clippings stick to my pants, which are already tacky from last night's garbage.

The mower keeps sticking in the thick patches until Desi, who knows about engines, finds an oil can in the shed and drips oil into the two tiny holes by the axle. Suddenly everything goes better. Desi's little brother, Philippe, rakes the long lines of fallen grass into neat rows away from the blades so we don't have to cut the same grass twice. We do not allow Philippe to work with the mowing team because I am scared he will get his sneakers caught in the blades, which go round and round like a ferris wheel. We have got the rhythm of it. We are working like a team.

Mrs. Jennings comes out of the house with sandwiches on a silver tray, a glass pitcher full of lemonade and ice cubes, and glasses. She sits down in the shade of the willows and talks to us, spreading her skirt out carefully on the freshly mowed grass. We gulp down the cool lemonade and eat cucumber sandwiches with the crusts cut off.

She went to school with my mom. She calls my mother Louisa. She laughs at Bubby chewing on the ice cubes after the lemonade is gone.

At last we put the mower back in the shed, sling the rope around the roller, and haul it clank-bump along the sidewalks. We are the envy of every kid in town. We strain our muscles, like the big horse-pulling teams at the Weymouth Fair, getting it over the railroad tracks and up the long hill to the Ballfield.

16

Catch-It-on-the-Bounce

I call Mr. Budd, but Mrs. Budd says he is putting in a well crock on North Noel Road, up the Shore. He will not be bringing clay this morning.

There is no chance of a real ball game, so I dig up Freddie and Bubby and half the French Street gang and we go up to the Ballfield to play catch-it-on-the-bounce. This is a good game to play when there are a lot of little kids.

The Tiger is shucking scallops off the Long Wharf. The draggers came in from George's Bank last night, and they are anchored off the Wharf. The strings of lights on their decks make the harbour look like Christmas. Even though the Tiger is our regular pitcher, I don't mind him working the odd day, because the last time the Tiger shucked scallops, he bought two new Spauldings with Warren Spahn's autograph on them. One of them got soaked in salt water when it went out in the tide under the Long Wharf, and tightened up into a hard, little nut. The other is still going strong.

Ronnie is down in the Café cutting up vegetables with his grandmother, but Mei-Ling has finished her chores and she comes along.

We don't really need the whole team for catch-it-on-the-bounce anyway, and I am anxious to try out the new outfield, as the sod has been laid down for three or four days now.

It looks beautiful. Just like a lawn, but flat and regular, so the bounce is true. I imagine what the Ballfield will look like once the infield is covered with clay and rolled. In my mind, it looks pretty good—like the big leagues.

We choose teams for catch-it-on-the-bounce, which you can play with any number of kids. Today we are eleven, six and five, so we take Philippe on our side as last choice to even it up.

In this game you throw the ball to the batter

underhanded. Everybody gets to bat, there are no called balls or strikes, and there is no umpire. The only way you can get out is to swing and miss three times or to hit a ball that someone catches in the air or on the first bounce.

Nobody ever told me these rules. It's just how you play catch-it-on-the-bounce.

Because the little kids—Desi's brother, Philippe, and René—are with us we decide not to use the stinger-miss rule that lets you drill a runner with the ball and sting him out. We will throw to the base instead.

We are using Mei-Ling's ball today; it used to be red, white, and blue stripes, but it is so old that the paint is all flaked off. Only the brown sponge inside is showing. It's the perfect ball to stinger-miss someone in the bare legs if you're a good shot.

The problem with drilling a little kid in the bare legs with a sponge ball is that it leaves a big, round red mark, and the next thing you know the kid's gone home crying, and you've got a mad mother marching up the street, and you all have to take off. The game is over.

This takes a lot of fun out of a rubber-ball game.

So we forget about stinger-miss, but all the other rules are in: No ball gloves allowed; ball goes in the grass, fielder yells "lost ball!" (even when he knows where it is), and all the runners have to freeze until the fielder bends down to pick it up; the team at bat has to supply a catcher; if there's an argument about whether you caught the ball on the first or second bounce, safe or out, it's settled by the captains, me and Desi.

I am not too keen on arguing over this kind of stuff with Desi, but if you don't yell a bit, your batter thinks you let him down.

We decide who bats first by Desi tossing me a bat, handle up, which I catch low down, and we put hands on it—first Desi's, then mine—until there is just enough room for the last guy to squeeze on two fingers and still twirl the bat around his head three times. If he doesn't drop it his team bats first.

We bat first. I've got little fingers.

Mei-Ling leads off. Desi tosses the ball across

the plate underhand and Mei-Ling gives it a hard undercut. The ball squirts up in front of her face, spins back after one bounce—a crazy, twirling back-spin, like a top going sideways—grounds in front of home plate, and goes foul into the backstop. Strike one.

The next pitch comes across the plate about neck high and Mei-Ling lets it pass. She likes low ones. I am catching for them and I chuck it back to Desi.

The third ball comes in about waist high and she takes a step in to meet it, foot in the bucket. The bat swings up from her heels, the barrel of the bat rocks into the sponge ball, and it soars in a high rainbow arc out toward left field. The outfielder sprints toward the spot where it will land. If he can get there in time to catch it on the first bounce, this blast is nothing but one long out.

The ball is too well hit for that and it bounces two or three strides beyond the fielder, soars again in another rainbow, and rolls into the outfield scrub beyond the new sod.

Mei-Ling is trotting home by the time the

ball is chucked back in to Desi. 1-0. It's an inside-the-park home run.

I am up next and Mei-Ling takes over as catcher.

As a joke, I lay a bunt down the first-base line. This is risky because a sponge ball can bounce two or three times straight toward the pitcher, who can simply pick it up on the last bounce and catch you out. But the ball lies down dead just off the mound and I am safe.

I am bent over first base getting my wind back when the Town truck pulls up and one of the Town workmen gets out, jumps across the ditch, and orders us off the field.

He stops to look at the roller, and then he says to me, because I am coming to meet him, "Where in the old bald-headed Moses did this come from?"

This is a pretty big man, and I don't know who he is, but he is wearing overalls that the Town gives out, and driving around in the Town truck. I say, "It's mine."

And it is, so I am going to stick to this.

The Town guy looks back at the driver and

points to the roller, but the driver shakes his head, "No, it doesn't belong to the Town." It is too much of a puzzle for him, so he gives up on it. He begins waving to the outfielders to come in, and yelling at them to get off the field.

I am waiting for this Town guy to drop dead from a lightning bolt out of the sky, because I know that if you use language like his, it is a ticket straight to everlasting fire.

Desi comes over, and because he is a lot taller than I am, the Town guy starts swearing at him instead of at me.

I back off because I am not sure how wide a lightning bolt is.

"Get those kids off that sod," the Town guy says to Desi. "We just put that down."

Nobody on our side says anything.

"Got to keep off it till we take the pegs out," he says.

I have noticed the pegs. There are little pegs stuck in the turf to keep it down until the roots take.

"What's that roller for?" he asks, going back to the roller.

The rest of the kids crowd around.

"We got clay coming," I say. "And then we're going to roll it."

The guy laughs and then begins yelling and swearing again, telling us there's no clay going on this field this year, we are not going to roll it, there's a fence going up to protect the sod, we are going to stay off it, and so on.

This is serious language he is using—I mean, serious curses. I am waiting for the thunderbolt!

Because none of us is moving, he picks up two ball gloves, which we weren't using because it is catch-it-on-the-bounce, and he chucks them at René, Desi's little brother's friend.

I am wishing that he had thrown them at Desi, because I know Desi could whip this bum.

Being more lippy than smart I tell the Town guy a ball game has nine innings and we are only in the first, which is not really true, because in catch-it-on-the-bounce you don't really have innings, and no one even bothers to keep track of the score.

"I know who you are," he says. I am not sure what this means.

"Who do you think you are," I say, looking at his overalls.

At this point the Town guy makes like he is going to grab me by the neck and sling me around, but I don't give a whiff, because I know Desi will haul him off.

The driver of the Town truck jumps out and tells this guy, Wendell, to calm down. I figure this must be Wendell's boss.

"We're going to be back here at noon," the dummy Wendell says, "and if this roller's not gone off this field, this guy is taking it off in that truck." He points at the "this" and the "that" every time he mentions it.

Then he sits down in the dugout and has a smoke, like he's not leaving until we do.

I decide to spare him a heart attack because he has a red face like Weird Willie Brush has, so I give him a dirty look and we leave.

We take the roller down the street and stash it in Tommy's shed. Tommy is the janitor at the brick school and a guy you can trust.

"Well, I guess we shouldn't've been on the grass yet," Freddie says.

"So he's got to yell and curse to get us off?" I say.

I am still wondering what he meant by saying he knows who I am. "How does he know who I am?"

"They just say that," Mei-Ling says. "He doesn't know who you are."

"How long does it take for grass to grow roots?" Bubby asks.

"A week," Desi says, but I am not sure if Desi knows this or if he is just trying to be helpful.

"Really?" I ask.

"It's sod," Desi says. "It's already got roots. If it rains, a week."

But it isn't really whether it is a week or a month. I can tell Mei-Ling is bothered too.

I know what she's thinking: Can a guy who doesn't play ball kick us off the Ballfield?

I can't even look at Mei-Ling and Desi because I know they want me to say or do something, and I don't know what to say, much less what to do. We all think up some excuse to leave and straggle off home when a few minutes ago we would have played ball half the day and even forgot lunch, it would have been that much fun.

17
The Tiger's Treehouse

My mom tells me she is tired and she doesn't have time to wash my pants tonight. She says I can wear my shorts tomorrow or wash my own pants. I know I could wash them but whenever I do, they end up too wet to dry by morning or with little soapy patches all over them. And I figure I can't wear shorts because tomorrow we are having a secret meeting in the Tiger's treehouse. I can't very well wear short pants to a secret meeting. I might as well go with lipstick on my face.

Once we made Howard's little brother, Randolph, do that. It was part of the torture to let him into the treehouse. It was supposed to look like blood, but it only made him look like a clown.

Finally my sister says I am being a pest. OK, she will wash my pants. This is a big relief! I have to promise to clean out the stove ashes and bring rain water in from the barrel so she can wash her hair. I sleep a lot better knowing I will have a pair of clean, dry pants to put on.

In the morning, I go first to the Cornwallis Café to see if Mei-Ling and Ronnie can come to the secret meeting. They are in the kitchen wearing big white aprons. It's easy to see why Ronnie is big, because there is food everywhere. Ronnie is standing by the sink cutting slivers off cooked chicken with a long, thin knife. Mei-Ling and her grandmother are over by the big wooden chopping block, chopping up vegetables with a meat cleaver.

Their dad will let them go if they can be back by noon for the lunch rush. They say they will. He gives me a hot egg roll wrapped in a white paper napkin to keep the sauce from burning my hand. I say thank you very slowly, as I don't know how well he understands English. He says the egg roll is for a "ball prayer," which is not too far from the truth.

"Your dad's a good guy for letting you come," I say to Ronnie, who is watching me zip up the egg roll inside my jacket pocket— for the Tiger.

"He likes us to play baseball," Mei-Ling says.

We pick up Freddie, although we have to wait for him to finish his breakfast. Freddie's mother does not work and she makes him eat breakfast with her every morning. Bubby is not home. He may be with the Tiger anyway. The Van Tassels and Howard and Randolph live out on Old Pit Lane, near the Tiger.

"We are having a meeting," I tell Mei-Ling, "in the Tiger's treehouse." I do not go into the details—it's understood that the meeting is about the Ballfield. It is also suspected that I don't know what to do about it. I am grateful that no one is pointing this out.

I have forgotten that Mei Ling is a girl, and she is not even allowed into the treehouse. I remember this when we are only halfway up Dairy Hill. We are so far along I don't know what to say to her, so I don't say anything. I don't even know if Mei-Ling knows the rule.

Geez, I've got problems!

"Nice day for a ball game," I say, at last. It *is* a nice day for a ball game. We are kicking up the dust as we walk. I see a few light clouds overhead, which is perfect, because then you don't lose the ball in the sun or get headaches round about the fourth inning. I love a cool, dry day.

The Tiger's treehouse is in his backyard, in an old apple tree that used to be part of an orchard. This tree is so old that it only has apples on it every second year. It is twisted and the branches are thick and go out in every direction, like an umbrella. The bark is rough and gives your sneakers a good hold, so it is pretty easy to climb.

The Tiger should really have a rope ladder. We tried making one out of rope that we found on the beach, but there's some special Brothers of the Spear rope-ladder knot that only the Brothers know and that stops the knots from slipping. We strung up the ladder and sent up Howard's little brother, Randolph. The knots slipped, and the rope caught Randolph around the ankle, flipping him over. We knew then that we had made a Brothers of the Spear antelope ankle trap, instead of a Brothers of the Spear rope ladder. Randolph hung upside down, which was OK because he hadn't made it very far up anyway. He had an ugly red wrist-burn on his ankle.

Since we could never figure out the rope-ladder secret, we nailed boards in a circle up and around the trunk to the first branch. You go around the trunk, and out of sight once you reach the treehouse. The Tiger made a trapdoor out of a barrel top with a stone on it, to keep people out when we are having a secret meeting.

The Tiger is already in the treehouse by the time we get there, and Mei-Ling climbs up around the trunk with the rest of us. The Tiger does not say a thing—no word of a lie.

Bubby is there too, and I can tell he is just as surprised as I am.

First I tell the Tiger about the Town workmen kicking us off the Ballfield. It seems pretty funny today, although it was scary yesterday.

"Desi was going to pop him one, the first move he made," Bubby says.

"Nicky asked him who he thought he was," Freddie says.

It gets funnier as we go along, and in the end we are too weak from laughing to figure out what to do about the Ballfield.

Altogether there are seven of us in the treehouse and I am wondering if this is one too many.

From a distance the treehouse looks sturdy, but when you get up close you can see that it is just some fish net, a door, two packing crates, and some boards. You have to pick your floorboard carefully because there are some rotten ones, just for looks. There are no chairs or anything, you just sit on the floor or on the tree limbs coming through. Seven is a lot of kids for a treehouse.

There's me—I am sitting on an old door lifted from the dump, and it is pretty solid. Mei-Ling and Ronnie make three. Nobody is sitting near Ronnie, in case he goes through the floorboards. The Tiger says that the fish net underneath the tree house is a snare to tangle anyone who tries to creep up while we are having a secret meeting, but as far as I am concerned, it is to catch Ronnie—if he goes through the floor.

The Tiger is perched on the tree limb which goes through the house. He looks safe there. Howard makes five. He's a skinny guy, so he's safe too. Freddie and Bubby make seven. They are just inside the door and if the whole thing collapses they can get out quickly.

The Tiger says he was sleeping out in this treehouse one time when he looked up and a bat the size of a chicken hawk came flying in, attached itself upside down to the tree limb and went to sleep. No word of a lie.

The treehouse is pretty high up, and that is the way bats sleep. How else would the Tiger know about it. He hasn't read *King Solomon's Mines* like I have.

There is a square hole, covered with plastic, in one wall, which is a look-out window. There is a hole in the floor which you come up through, and a small hole in the ceiling which is an emergency exit, like in the theatre. If the tree is burning, the roof hole will let you get higher up. According to the Tiger, this hole is for the stove he is going to move in, so he can sleep out here during the winter, when there are no mosquitoes.

The more we talk, the more we laugh, and the more the treehouse shakes.

"We should have just ignored him and kept on playing," Howard says. "You know, just kept on playing."

"That only works on a hockey pond," I say. "They won't get on the ice to kick you off."

"We should have tackled him, let Ronnie sit on him," Bubby says. This is very funny and we laugh a lot at the idea of Ronnie sitting on the bum. Ronnie doesn't seem to mind the joke.

There is some serious discussion mixed in with the joking, and the general drift of it is that we should wait until the turf has taken root. Then we can go back and play ball.

"Desi says it will only be a week."

"What does he know?"

"Yeah, his father's a fisherman."

"Desi knows."

A meeting in a treehouse is always a good thing. You get a chance to joke, clown around, talk things over, and see what the other guy has got.

The Tiger has got some good stuff from somewhere—a whole lot of steel ball bearings. A ball bearing is the ultimate marble. I bet he got these from the machine shop, when he was shucking scallops. He also has a new bunch of baseball cards, including a Joe Adcock and a Del Crandall, which will complete my Braves collection, if I can get them. Also he has a secret weapon that none of us has ever seen before in anybody's treehouse. I have seen BB guns, Red Ryders and Johnny Mack Browns, home made bows and arrows, and slingshots made out of alder forks and rubber from inner tubes, but the Tiger has added a new weapon to the arsenal. He has ten big red balloons filled with water in a cardboard box.

"What are those water balloons for?" I ask the Tiger. "Girls," he says. Mei-Ling laughs.

Suddenly I figure it out. We will play our home games for the time being down on the Cannonbanks. I will ask Desi if this is OK with him. I figure it will be OK, because we have a game coming up with South End that Desi would like to see. Maybe we will be short a guy and he can play. I can't promise he can play—just hint at it.

I really want to play South End again because they are the best team, and we have only beaten them once this year—the rain game, with five innings. Now that we have Mei-Ling regular at short, we are a lot stronger up the middle.

I wish we could have Desi play for us all the time, but that would leave French Street short. What a team that would be, with Desi, the Tiger and Mei-Ling! The Raven All-Stars. The All-Star Ravens. Nicky Come-Play-Ball, Captain, Manager.

I am dreaming up a whole new line-up when Mei-Ling and Ronnie say they have to get back to the Café. This breaks up the meeting.

The guys are clearing out and I ask Ronnie

and Mei-Ling, Freddie and Bubby to wait for me under the tree. Ronnie knows I still have the hot egg roll.

When we are alone, I say to the Tiger, "Give you this egg roll for your Joe Adcock and Del Crandall." I bring out the egg roll.

The Braves are not the Tiger's team anyway, so I figure the Tiger will go for the deal. He has a double on Crandall, the Braves' catcher. So he is really only giving up the Joe Adcock, right?

"You got any Yankees?" he says.

"When I get Yankees cards," I say, "I give them to my sister; she cuts them up to do her hair."

The Tiger does not think this is funny, but he really wants the egg roll, so he gives me the two cards and I promise him the first Yankee card I get. I tuck Crandall and Adcock into my clean pocket and try to wipe the grease out of the other one with what's left of the paper napkin. The Tiger devours the egg roll in two gulps.

My mom always says to chew your food fifty times. I hope this will not make him too sick to play ball.

I run backward down the tree trunk, thinking of the two cards in my pocket. Ronnie looks at my greasy pocket and knows the egg roll is gone. I show him the two cards, but he's too hungry to care about baseball cards.

I can imagine what he is going to do to the first half-eaten plate of fish and chips that comes back from the dining room of the Cornwallis Café.

Just a few steps beyond the tree trunk, Ronnie takes a water balloon in the back of the neck. It explodes on impact, *ka-sploosh!* What a bomb!

Two more come down, but we are running now, and they miss and hit the ground, bursting open and splashing the dry dust. I laugh. I don't feel mad about the Tiger doing this. I'd do it.

When you've got a treehouse and ten red water balloons and a target, what else are you going to do?

18
Saturday's Game

Saturday is a great day for a ball game. You can play any time you want because no one is doing anything else, and you get a good crowd out too.

I have fixed it up with Desi to play at the Cannonbanks and I have asked South End if we can start the game a little late, around two o'clock. This is OK with South End because they have played French Street at the Cannonbanks before, and they understand that I do not want any more lost balls off the right field line, floating out under the Wharf. If we play at two, the tide is out, and the foul balls will just land in the mud.

Half of French Street is here to watch us play, including Desi, because we have the full line-up. We even have one Van Tassel to spare.

I take myself out of the game, and sub Howard's little brother, Randolph, who is turning into a pretty fair ballplayer. Being coach and manager at the same time gives me lots to do, and besides, last time up I got called out on strikes. The ball was way off the plate, but Walter called it a strike. I left Dougie Van Tassel stranded on third base with the score 4-2 for South End going into the tail end of the ball game.

The Tiger has been throwing wild today, and South End have got their runs on balls, walks, and the odd scratch single. I think it's the crowd. The Tiger wants to be a power pitcher and he forgets that you can get an out with one ground ball to Mei-Ling at short. He is throwing six or seven pitches to every batter, mostly high fastballs, because when he gets wild he throws high.

One of his high balls went over the batter's head and hit Walter the Umpire, who fortunately is protected in every possible location. Spindly Walter went down in a heap like a black coal sack down a chute. Even though Walt wasn't hurt, and jumped up quickly, it is not a good thing to bean the umpire, even though the crowd kind of likes it. You may need a close call to go your way in the last innings of the game.

The Tiger is steaming and puffing now, so I walk out to the mound to calm him down. If the Tiger can settle down and we can make up a run somehow, we are back in the game. On the other hand, if they score one now, we will lose heart, and the game is over. Mei-Ling and Ronnie come out too—that is the most people you can have on the mound.

We are having this little chat with the Tiger when Walter comes to out break it up, calling us gentlemen and asking us to "get on with the game."

Mei-Ling hangs back and tells the Tiger that the next batter is left-handed, which he is—it's Bell, who has hit the Tiger before—and to keep the ball low and inside.

This is the first time I have ever heard Mei-Ling speak to the Tiger, other than to say hi, so

I am surprised. I have never told the Tiger where to throw the ball.

First pitch—the Tiger puts it low on the inside corner, which jams Bell a bit. He can't get the bat around, and the ball squirrels off weakly toward second base, an easy catch for Randolph, who we have nicknamed Shrimp. He tosses it to Bubby for the second out.

This gives the Tiger confidence, and I can see he is getting pumped up to strike out the next guy, when Mei-Ling begins to chatter. You know, the regular kind of stuff, "Atta boy, good pitch.... Way to chuck it in there."

This next guy, Perry, is a good hitter. I don't know his last name, but he bats right-handed. The Tiger glances over at Mei-Ling and then deals low and outside. Although Perry connects pretty good, the ball is a big hopper heading straight to Mei-Ling. This is so much like her India-rubber-ball routine that I smile even before the ball is in her glove. She takes it with both hands, plants her left foot, and whips the ball to first—so quick and straight you could have hung clothes on it.

In fact, it is so quick and straight it surprises Bubby. The ball hits his first baseman's mitt and pops out, but Bubby picks it up fast and makes the out. Walter has run down the first base line alongside Perry, so there is no argument there.

Third out ... two outs on two pitches! End of the inning.

This low and outside, low and inside stuff is a major discovery for the Tiger. I can tell when he comes in that he is thinking about it. Thinking does not come easy for him—it screws up his face. I hope he is thinking he can use this on the rest of the guys when he absolutely needs to— say, when the bases are loaded. He will be showing them something new.

This is what I think, but I'm only the manager. Why should he listen to me?

Unfortunately this is the high point of the game for us. We are only able to scratch up one more run on a bunt single by Freddie—two long fly-outs put him on third, and the Tiger's crack double to left field brings him home. Howard strikes out on account of being nervous. We lose 4-3. It's a big game, it's a big loss, but it's early in the season.

Walter congratulates us all on a very sportsmanlike game, insisting on shaking hands all round. He has to bend over from the waist to reach Randolph, who we now call Shrimp. He puts his clicker in his chest pocket, which has flaps and buttons on it. I thank him on behalf of the Ravens, apologize for the Tiger hitting him, and tell him I have no hard feelings over his calling me out on strikes. Walter waves away my comment about hard feelings and strides off, looking like a kid on stilts. You'd think he was the Prince of Wales, but I want to tell you, there's a guy who knows how to ump a ball game.

Losing 4-3 means we are 1 and 2 against South End this year, which puts us way over last year when we were 0 and 3. This is going to be *some* year. We have added Mei-Ling at short, and Shrimp coming along at second really makes the infield tight. If the Tiger smartens up and uses his infield, no one will touch him.

We could win this thing. We could have beaten South End. We could go on....

I am telling Bell that it will not be much longer before we can use our ballfield, and that we are getting real clay for the infield when Desi comes over from the sidelines. He wants to set up a game between French Street and South End. The coach for South End comes over too, so Bell, his coach, Desi and me are all standing there.

"There're no more games with you guys," Bell says.

I am not sure, with Desi there, whether "you guys" means us, the Ravens, or Desi and French Street. Or both.

"You guys," he says, nodding toward Desi and me. He means both.

No more games?

19
A Showdown with Fosdick

I haven't got the faintest idea what Bell is talking about. Some of the other South End guys come up too, and some of the Ravens. It's hard to figure something out when everybody is talking at the same time. Anyway, this guy we call Fosdick, who is South End's coach, tries to shout everybody down.

We named him Fosdick because he looks like Fearless Fosdick's girlfriend in the comics. He has a very sharp chin, like an axe. He is mostly bald but has little tufts of red hair around his ears. He is the first guy I have ever seen with freckles on top of his head.

Fosdick is upset all the time, so we don't talk to him much. Mainly we talk to Bell because he was the South End captain before Fosdick came along with the van.

We call this guy Fosdick behind his back. Fosdick is a nickname like the Tiger and Nicky Come-Play-Ball. But we don't mind our names.

While the South End guys are trying to tell the Ravens what is happening, I am quizzing Bell and getting edgy because I know this has something to do with the Ballfield. South End's coach is trying to drown everybody out, so I say, "Fosdick, shut up a minute, will ya?"— which is not what you say to a grown-up if you have any sense.

I know I have made a big mistake here, because he turns three shades of red. Is it my imagination or do I see little sparks jumping from one tuft of hair to the other, across his bald head. He is sizzling!

"What did you call me?" he asks.

You have to understand that most of the time, when we play ball, there are no grown-ups around, except for Walter the Umpire, and he is like one of the team. If we disagree with his call—like in the last game when he called me out on strikes and I told him owls see better in the daytime than he does, that is all part of the ball game.

When Tommy the Janitor fishes a broken bat out of the garbage for us, glues it, puts a little screw in the handle, and wraps it up with black tape, someone will say, "Gee, thanks," but that doesn't mean Tommy will stick around and make a nuisance of himself telling us how we should play the game. He might play an inning himself, for the fun of it, or show you something, like the double steal, but he isn't bossy, and you can say anything to him you like.

But this guy Fosdick is bossy, and South End is not as much fun to play with since he came around. I have made a big mistake letting his nickname out of the bag.

Either I have to take it back, or I have to say it again.

I take it back.

"I'm sorry, sir," I say, "I thought your name was Foster." This gets a big laugh. I don't need a big laugh right now.

"My name to you is Morine. Mr. Morine."

"Yes, sir."

"And Mr. Bell is correct."

I am wondering why he calls the South Enders Mister, since they are the same age we are, when he interrupts my thoughts. "As Mr. Bell has been saying, we won't be playing you fellows anymore, unless you are registered with the Town."

"I don't get it," I say, because I *don't* get it.

"Listen, Shorty," and now he is trying to pin me with a nickname, "you and your players have to register with the Town. There will be four teams sponsored by the merchants. You people register and you will be put on a team, and you'll get a uniform. The Town League starts next week, when the Ballfield is ready. You got that?"

I would really like for him to go through it again, but he is implying I am pretty slow if I don't get it the first time. What I do understand is bad enough, so I don't say anything.

I am glad to see that Mei-Ling, who is sharper on this stuff than I am, is taking it all in.

Then Fosdick asks, "Didn't your father tell you about this?"

This doesn't hurt, because I can't even

remember my dad now, but it gives me a good shot. "No, we don't talk much."

This gets a laugh from the Ravens, who know, but Fosdick thinks I am just trying to be lippy. He's right.

I don't want you to think my mom brought me up saucy. Somewhere along the way, I just started getting lippy, and now I can't stop it. When it comes out, it's out.

"You little punks don't deserve to play a real team anyway," Fosdick says. This is pretty weak, we think. We are 1 and 2 against South End this year, and it was a good ball game today.

Fosdick decides we are not worth talking to, and he goes off to load the bases into the van. I wonder what this guy does for a living and why he is hanging around us.

I turn back to Bell, who is a straight shooter. Bell is old for a kid, but he's still a kid. He likes to play ball.

"True?" I ask.

"True," he says.

I nod my thanks to Bell because I can see in

his eyes that he feels bad about it.

"Good game," I say.

"Good game."

We are walking home when the Tiger says, "What a moron." He means Fosdick.

Howard says, "Mr. Moron to you."

This gets the best laugh of the day.

20
The Town Clerk

I am supposed to be meeting the gang. We are off to the Grill for a swim. I should probably be heading out there right now, but I have an idea.

The Town Hall is downtown, just around the corner from the Cornwallis Café. I know because my mom sends me down there to pay the water bills. It's easy. You walk up to the counter and give the girl the slip and the money. It is usually about six dollars, depending upon how many baths my sister has been taking. The girl at the counter gives you a receipt.

My idea is to ask the girl about the Ballfield. She works for the Town, so she should know.

I walk up the stairs at the Town Hall, because the office part is on the second floor. The first floor is just a big empty storage room where they keep the town equipment, like old parking meters and street lamps. It's all must and dust. My mom could do something in there.

At the counter where you pay your bills, there is a big brass clock on the wall, which keeps the official Town time, and tells them when to blow the Town whistle. There are a lot of wooden pigeonhole boxes and maps on the walls. There are offices out back made of frosted glass like our bathroom window at home.

I am asking the woman at the counter about the Ballfield, when she says, "Oh, you'll want these." She gives me a form to fill out about playing in the Town Paperweight Baseball League. It is all typed up on a typewriter. It must be the truth.

"What is the Paperweight League?" I ask.

"Why, that's the league for you young sprouts," she says. And when I still don't get it, she says, "You know, a paperweight. It's a little thing you put on your desk to keep the papers from blowing away." She has a nice laugh, but I don't see anything funny. I mean, it is some kind of joke.

"We're handing out the forms at Cubs and Scouts," she says very friendly and politely because she sees I don't get the name, "but you can take some along if you want."

"I'm not in Scouts," I say, "or Cubs."

I realize now why the South Enders are all signed up already. They have Cubs and Scouts, which none of us Ravens are in. I don't think I am in this Paperweight League, either, but I don't tell her this.

I can see the Town clerk getting up from behind his desk, like a shadow, behind the frosted glass windows. He is coming out because he hears us talking at the counter. He is friendly and polite behind his spectacles— not glasses, but spectacles with wire rims, like your grandfather's.

He starts to explain the rules, only slower than Fosdick Moron did yesterday.

"Anybody can play, any kid in town," the clerk begins, and he smiles a friendly warm smile, for which I am grateful, because I didn't expect to be talking to the Town clerk. I was only geared up to talk to the woman who

takes the water bills, and I am way more nervous now. I wonder why I am nervous when someone is trying to be helpful, and lippy when they're not.

Then I realize that while he is smiling and trying to be helpful, he has just kicked Howard off the team. Howard is off because he lives near Old Pit Lane, in a little clump of shacks we call Moutonville, and that is in the County. There's a sign which says County right at the end of the lane. That's where the Town ends. That's where Howie and his brother, Randolph, nicknamed Shrimp, live.

"What if you live out of Town?" I say.

"Where do you live?"

"King Street."

"Well, I guess King Street's within the Town limits," the clerk says, smiling at my ignorance. The worry must be showing on my face because the clerk says again, "Any kid can play—age nine to thirteen."

I nod to show him I understand, but I wish I was brave enough to ask about Howard. At the same time, I really do know the answer, because Howard's mother does not send him down here to pay the Town water bills. So Howard and Shrimp are out for good. I feel like a bird caught in a trap.

My arms are going weak! It is like standing at home plate, being struck out on strikes, without even trying to swing the bat. I tell myself, "Come on! This is important! It's for everybody! Get with it!"

"But we already got a team," I say.

"You will be put on a team," the clerk says.

I don't want this guy to think I am stupid. But I can't say anything—I *am* just too confused.

"Now, how old are you, son?" the Clerk says quietly.

"Twelve," I squeak.

"Good," he says, "you can play this year and next year. You're safe."

"What if you're thirteen now," I ask, "and you turn fourteen in the summer?"

"It depends on when your birthday falls," the clerk says. The playoffs will be in August, so you've got to still be thirteen in August, but you could be fourteen, say, at the end of August. But you're OK. Don't worry."

The Tiger is thirteen right now. He is going on fourteen. I know because he has been bragging about it. Gee ... Desi. I wonder how old Desi is. I never thought to ask. This is a very kind and reassuring man; he is trying his best ... but the more he tells me, the worse it gets.

"Any boy, say, thirteen this summer, is eligible," he says.

There goes Mei-Ling. *There goes Mei-Ling!* Even though I am a little slow, I realize Mei-Ling is no boy. I may be slow, but I'm not stupid, and what I want to say is, "How about *girls*, if they have been playing?"

Instead I say, "OK."

"All games will be on the Ballfield," the clerk says. "We are laying down sod. We have spent over four thousand dollars already, approved by the Town. Each team will have a minimum of one game a week. Four teams— and new uniforms sponsored by the merchants.

You'll be getting a new uniform."

"No I won't," I think.

"The Town has approved another one thousand for the field," he says. Every time he tells me a rule he points his finger at the typewriting on the form.

He goes on with the rest of the rules. The registration is a buck a person. Your mom or your dad has to sign the form. I don't really hear the rest because my mind is racing off and away while I am standing there, nodding my head and saying, "OK."

"Wait," he says, laughing, "you need this," and he hands me a paper across the counter.

"No, I don't need that," I say. "Thank you."

The clerk gives the woman a "why did he make me go through all this if he didn't want to play ball" look. She gives him a "can you beat that " look. They both go back to work.

I look up at the brass clock on the wall. I must get down to the Grill before they all think I'm not going to show up, and take off. I have a real inspiration. I am nervous now, not from being scared—which I was nervous from before—but nervous from the thrill of what we've got to do.

As soon as I get away from the clerk and his frosted-glass office I can feel my spirits coming back. It is great to be outdoors. It is a beautiful day, and I want to go swimming down at the Grill. I want to see my friends. I want to play ball!

Suddenly I know we are going to win this thing. I can feel my spirits rising inside my chest. I feel my strength returning. I know that trying hard will not be good enough for the Ravens. We've got to win! *We will win!*

Let's go!

21

The Sawmill Meeting

On the way down the hill through the pines, heading toward the Grill, I see the Tiger and the rest of the gang are out of the water. They have finished swimming and are sitting out on the planks of the old sawmill above the run.

This is our favorite place to dry off. You can take off your shirt and hang it up to dry on the nails on the side of the mill. There are a thousand loose nails popping out where the sun's heat has split the grey planks.

The big saws and winches are lying around, rusted and dull, and the wooden wheels that look like big pieces of clockworks have fallen apart and are lying in piles where somebody stacked them.

You can sit there as long as you want because nobody cares about this old place anymore—except maybe the kingfishers, sitting on limbs over the water. This is a good place for kingfishers—the mill pond above and the race below are full of little trout and eels.

I see the Tiger sitting on the end of a plank, his feet dangling in the water.

"Hey, Tiger," I call. He looks around, but can't see me. I am still in the shadow of the pine trees. I move and he spots me.

The Tiger raises a hand to say, "I see you."

I slip around the back of the sawmill. There is a pile of sawdust there higher than the mill itself, and you can climb the pile and get above the mill. No one can hear you coming; the sawdust is too soft. I am careful not to make a sound as I slip around the mill. I see the Tiger here and there through the cracks in the boards. He has his head cocked to one side, following my progress.

I am in the sawdust pile, climbing to the top. My feet sink in up to my ankles. When I get to the top I can see everybody below, sunning on the grey planks, laid out like nine fish: the Tiger, Mei-Ling, Ronnie, Howard and his brother Randolph, Freddie and Bubby, Dougie Van Tassel, and Jimmy Christmas. The Ravens—win or lose, the best ballteam you ever saw!

I hold my arms out like a bird and shout "Banzai!" for all I am worth. When they all look up, I take a flying jump off the sawdust pile, turning one full loop in the air—over and down, head over tea kettle.

On landing, I am half buried. I have something sticking up my pantleg—probably bark ... and sawdust is very tough stuff to spit out of your nose.

I have seen the Lighthouse Road guys do this and they all do it better. You can believe it.

"Where've you been?" Howard asks.

"Yeah, where you been?" says Howard's little brother, Randolph. This little shrimp is getting lippy too, now that he takes a regular turn at bat.

"I've been down to the Town office," I say. I look at Howard and the Tiger and Mei-Ling; three great ballplayers who are all out—according to the Town clerk. They are standing apart from Freddie and Bubby and the others, like they know they are supposed to be apart. But they don't look any different to me.

I tell them the clerk's story of the new baseball league, and who's in and who's out.

"They've got it all written down?" Ronnie asks.

"Yeah, on a typewriter," I say.

"Well then, that's the way it is," Ronnie says. "Nothing we can do about it."

Ronnie is like that. He asks a question and then he goes along with whatever the answer is, right then and there.

Mei-Ling is different. She doesn't say anything for a long time. She just listens. The Tiger does not speak, even when I say the Town clerk says he is too old.

Howard is really embarrassed because his house is in the wrong place.

"But I've got an idea," I say.

"For starters, if the Tiger's too old, then so's Desi," I say. That sinks in.

"So's Phil—he's fourteen," Freddie says. Phil plays for South End. We all know he is fourteen because he has had to repeat two grades in school.

"French Street won't play without Desi," I say. "Gee, there are two or three on French Street that are under nine. Half those guys don't even make the League."

"Lighthouse Road is in the County," Bubby says. "I know, I used to live there."

"So we're not joining," I say. "We're the Ravens. Those guys will stick with us."

I see the Tiger nod his head. The Tiger is sitting on his heels like a catcher, sifting sawdust through his hands, but he is listening.

"We are the Outlaw League," I say, "And we play on the Ballfield."

"They'll kick us off," Bubby says.

"We'll come back. There's no fence around it."

"Pontiacs only play on the weekends, and those guys in the new league are only going to play one game a week."

"We'll get Desi and French Street."

"Lighthouse Road."

"Phil off South End."

"And Floyd—he's fourteen in July."

"We'll dye our uniforms black," I say, "all black. We'll stick together and play ball, and I bet Walter will ump' for us. He won't ump' for them, I bet."

"Nicky, you talk to him."

Mei-Ling says the next game is the only important one. It doesn't matter who is eleven now and who is thirteen later. If we want to play we should, and everybody that wants to play ball can play with us. She says if we want to dye our uniforms black, she can get the big pot from the Café as long as we can get it clean again. I say I can get the black dye from the hotel where my mom works.

"We've got to swear an oath," Howard says.

So we each swear and then make it binding—

we dip our fingers in the mud along the bank and draw a big black "R" on our foreheads.

"We are the Ravens—the Ravens of the Outlaw League."

"Yes," the Tiger says. This is the first time the Tiger has said anything.

"We are the Ravens," I say.

22
The Outlaw League

It takes about four days to organize the Outlaw League. Actually it is a lot like our old league, so it isn't that much to organize. We have the Ravens (Captain, me), French Street (Captain, Desi), Indian Hill (Captain, Lorry), Lighthouse Road (Captains, Brian and David).

Floyd and Bell from South End are playing for French Street, because they live closest to them. That makes French Street a pretty power-packed club, but the Tiger can handle them.

I am captain and coach and manager of the Ravens. Shrimp plays second base regular, and I sub in around the middle innings, and pinch hit. To tell you the truth, I am not such a hot ballplayer anyway.

Walter the Umpire is going to ump our games. He says they can't keep us off the Ballfield. It is for the kids of the Town and as long as we are kids we can play there. He will tell that to anybody who tries to kick us off.

We take a day to go up and spread out the clay around the infield. Then we give it two days to settle, roll it with Mrs. Jennings' roller, wet it, roll it again—and now we are ready to play our first double-header.

It's Friday morning, top of the first. The Tiger is taking his warming pitches—all fastballs.

Freddie catches the last one, pop, into his glove, and chucks the ball in a high loop down to second. Shrimp picks it up on the one-hop— the throw being a little short, but on the line— flips the ball to Mei-Ling, who is covering second base; she throws it back to the Tiger on the mound.

All four teams in the Outlaw League are here. We are playing French Street in the first game; Lighthouse Road is on with Indian Hill in the second.

Walter the Umpire is very excited because he feels he is in on baseball history. It's the first game of the Outlaw League, and he looks like a big, grand scarecrow. His arms sweep out above the batter and he calls out, "Play ball!"

It looks as if we are actually going to play this game without anybody coming to kick us off.

Desi sends up two little kids first, with strict instructions not to swing at anything.

The Tiger gets frustrated because they have such small strike zones and Walter is calling them exactly. The Tiger walks the first batter on four pitches, and the second on five, all fastballs.

OK, they have a man on first and a man on second when Desi steps up. The Tiger unloads and Desi cracks a double to right field, not quite getting around on it. By the time Howard gets it back in, both runners have scored. We don't have an out yet, and Bell is batting fourth for them.

We get a lot of razzing from Indian Hill and Lighthouse Road. They are laughing it up, and

I have to admit we are not off to a good start. Still, there are nine innings in a ball game.

I walk out to the mound to settle the Tiger down. The Tiger looks pretty good in his all-black uniform. We've got to get black caps, I think—but the Tiger won't wear anything but a Yankee's cap.

I stand on top of the mound with the Tiger, and look around. The Ballfield looks great, just the way I thought it would. It looks just like the majors with the red clay on the infield rolled smooth, and the green grass covering the outfield. Above is a pale-blue sky that says sunshine all day today and tomorrow too.

The Tiger is not upset. He knows that I am not going to take him out. He just needs a breather to calm down.

"We need three outs," I say, which is not very bright, but sometimes it's hard to think of the right thing to say.

"Low and outside," Mei-Ling whispers. "Low and outside."

I didn't even see her come up to the mound.

I look over at the batter. It's Bell.

"Yeah, low and outside," I say.

"Condemned," the Tiger says. "This guy's condemned-to-die."

The Tiger is pretty well settled down and I think he will start working the plate, in and out. We are in for a pretty good ball game now....

Then the Town truck pulls up, and the big dummy Wendell in the blue overalls who hassled us before gets out and jumps across the drainage ditch. He has long legs and big boots. The boots make him taller.

"Oh oh, here he comes! This is it," I think. Either I'm chicken for the rest of my life, or I take a licking and go down swinging. There's no other way out.

Wendell comes to the edge of the field, where we have put down white lime for lines, and he scuffs a line with his boot.

I step in front of him. I'm not scared. I was before I moved, but when I stepped in front of him my fear went away.

"Who the blue blazes do you think you are?" he yells.

"Same guy I was this time last week," I say.

This is not my best shot, but maybe I can think up better stuff as we go along. Wendell looks back to the Town truck, with a sarcastic "will you look at this little twirp" look.

I think maybe I have this guy on the ropes because he can't actually hit me with everybody here, so I'm not moving unless he does.

"You little twirps don't have permission to play here," he says, "so off you go."

"We've been playing here since before you started working for the Town."

"I don't have to stand here talking to you," he says.

"Nobody's stopping you from leaving," I say. This is an old standard. Surely I can think of better stuff than this.

"We put four thousand bucks in this field," the big dummy Wendell says, "and you kids come out here—running on it."

"My mom's taxes paid for it," I say. "They pay you too."

You can tell when somebody wants to hit you. When they are going to pop you one, you can tell exactly when it's going to come. It's coming now.

Wendell draws back his hand…. Then the driver of the Town truck yells, "Wendell, take it easy for crying out loud!"

Wendell gives me the worst "I'll see you later, you little twirp" look—and heads back to the truck. The truck roars away towards Town.

I am still shaking because I know I have come *this* close to getting clobbered. That Wendell doesn't know what you can do to a kid and what you can't. That is something grown-ups have to know, the same as we have to know what you can say to a grown-up.

I have just started to calm down, thinking that maybe that's the last we'll see of the guy today, and the game can go on … when the Town truck comes back again.

Geez, they've brought the Town clerk this time! I remember all that typewriting the Town clerk showed me down at the Town Hall. I know this is something I can't get past just by being lippy and taking a smack in the mouth.

The Town clerk doesn't jump across the drainage ditch. He walks down around the path and up behind home plate, with the big dummy Wendell in the overalls following him.

"See," Wendell says, "they're playing ball."

The Town clerk takes his spectacles out of the case as if he is going to read the fine print on something he has in his shirt pocket, rather than look at a baseball field. He begins polishing his spectacles with his handkerchief. He looks out at the field. I get the idea this is the first time he has been up here since we rolled out the clay. He takes a look around and sees the mound we have built up—and the white base lines. He looks at the players on the field and the players in the dugouts.

Wendell says again, "They're playing ball."

"Yes," says the Town clerk, "so they are."

Then he nods at me. He remembers me from the visit I paid to his office. He does not say a blessed thing more. There is a great silence. He turns and walks back to the truck.

The next thing I hear is the Tiger saying, "Attaway, Nicky Come-Play-Ball."

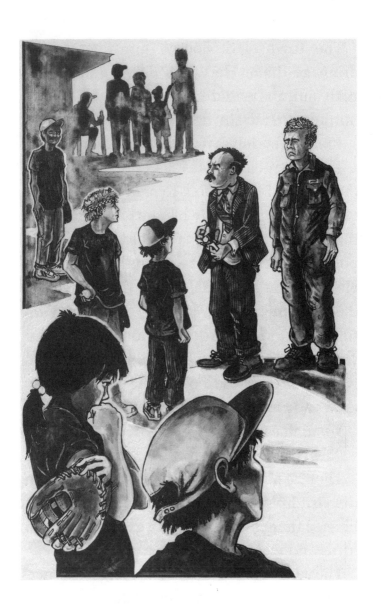

Now I know that we will play ball the way we always have—with all the fun of the game today and the hope of a game tomorrow. And I know too that from now on we've only got to think about the rules of baseball—no other rules!

The clerk leaves, riding back to the Town office in the Town truck, with the big dummy Wendell sitting out back on the box, because there is only room for the driver and the clerk in the cab.

The Tiger picks the ball out of his glove and the ball hangs beside him, held loosely in his fingers. He is ready to burn one in there.

I look over at Mei-Ling at short, and I give her a look that says, "hey, do you see what's happening?"

She gives me back a look, "yes, yes—isn't it great?"

Geez, this is incredible—I am about to see the Tiger throw his first curveball!